Driftwood

Driftwood

AMIT K CHOUDHURY

PARTRIDGE
A Penguin Company

FT
Pbk

Partridge books may be ordered through booksellers or by contacting:

Partridge India
Penguin Books India Pvt.Ltd
11, Community Centre, Panchsheel Park, New Delhi 110017
India
www.partridgepublishing.com
Phone: 000.800.10062.62

ACKNOWLEDGEMENT

I hesitantly had asked some of my colleagues for their opinion on a short story I had written. The unanimous verdict was:

"You must expand this into a novel. This is too short and unsatisfactory."

Thus was born the concept of 'Driftwood'. With urgings from my colleagues, and encouragement I ventured on my maiden voyage of storytelling. I am most grateful to Leni Littleton for her patience to read through my early manuscript, her suggestions and encouragements. Achyut Guleri pushed me for publication of this novel.

Writing is a lonely business; however I had received suggestions, help and encouragement from too many to name. I apologise to them for the omission. I am grateful to the publishing team at Partridge publications, for their help and support, especially Ann Minoza and Dia Mercado.

I am indebted to the silver jubilee magazine of the Border Roads Organisation for its factual history and anecdotes.

I am grateful to various websites on Garhwal that provided me with the facts and figures to embellish on my own experiences. www.hinduism.za is a rich resource.

This book is a work of fiction, and should be treated as such. All characters are fictitious, and any resemblance is coincidental. I have tried to bring up some aspects of the present Indian society, especially with the breaking down of the joint family structure there is no anchor or safety net. Each of us is in danger of becoming driftwood in the stream of life.

Shortcomings of this book are due to my limitations as a writer.

Last but not the least I am grateful to all my readers for reading this book.

DEDICATION

I dedicate this book to the men and women of the Border Roads Organisation whose efforts under difficult conditions keep the sub-Himalayan states of India connected.

RAJIV

The telephone receiver slipped off my slack fingers, hit the wall and started to swing like a pendulum. I was paralysed. I could see and hear and smell the university cafeteria, but my brain refused to register any information. It could not be true!

An urgent summon had brought me to the telephone, interrupting my dinner. The call was from one of my father's colleagues and close family friend, Jayant. I have known him all my life. He asked me on the phone to pack my bags and come home as soon as possible. Both my parents were involved in a car accident and were in critical care unit of the local hospital.

I was a second year mechanical engineering student in the Indian Institute of Technology, at Kanpur: living in the college hostel. My father was a professor of biochemistry at the University College of Delhi, and lived in the campus. He had recently bought a Maruti-Suzuki car and was quite proud of it. Kanpur was only six hours from Delhi by train, and being on the main line, connections were frequent.

I walked back to my table like a zombie. My friends realised something was wrong; I told them. I did not have much money on me, and they arranged a collection. They helped me to pack my bag and one of them gave me a lift on his Yezdi motorbike to the railway station, bought my ticket and put me on the first available train going to Delhi. He gave me the rest of the money they had collected, in case of emergency. I probably did thank them, I do not remember. Having no reservation, I had to push my way into the unreserved compartment, and settled near the door, using my bag as a seat. The guard blew his whistle and the train rushed off into the night. I tried desperately not to think the worst.

The rhythmic roll of the train and the monotonous clanging of wheels on steel rails had a mesmerising effect. I gazed out of the open door; breeze generated by the fast moving train ruffled my hair and cooled my face. Overall the atmosphere had a soothing effect on my anxiety, the fear of the impending disaster.

The more I tried to steer my thoughts away from my parents, the more my thoughts seemed to stick to memories of my childhood and adolescence, time spent with my parents. The good times we had and the punishments I received. I could not escape feeling their overwhelming love for me, their only son. I was the centre of all their endeavours and aspirations. A kaleidoscope of events unrelated in time and space flitted through in front of my eyes, unseeing yet with vivid clarity. I was six years old in my primary school, running a fifty-metre race on the sports day. I ran through the tape straight into my mother's arms. How proudly she showed off my first trophy to all our friends and neighbours.

I was ten and on the stage, receiving prizes for general proficiency and over all merit scholarship for being first in my class. I received the prize, bowed and turned to go back to my seat. I saw my mother wiping her eyes, with my father's arm around her shoulder. I was in an inter-school cricket match. I was batting. I hit a front foot drive and saw the ball racing towards the boundary. I ran, and then it was over. I had hit the winning run. I was selected for the state school cricket team. I received a warm hug from my father and a word of encouragement from him.

We were playing catch me if you can, and Vijay was chasing me. I climbed a guava tree. It had a leaning branch that led on to a high wall. My plan was to run along the wall, and then jump off where the sand for the new construction was piled high against the wall. Unfortunately my feet slipped and I fell off the wall. I broke my wrist. I remember the anxious faces of my parents as they took me to the hospital. We waited. Then I was under anaesthesia, and when I woke up I had a plaster over my forearm. My mother was smiling, but she had tears in her eyes. Later I had a high fever and severe headache. I was restless and could not sleep. My mother was sponging me. She stayed up most of the night till I fell asleep.

I was in a lead role, presenting a play in our annual school function. I forgot my words. I smiled and nodded my head trying desperately to remember. I took a turn, and walked the length of the stage, as if pensive. I looked up and caught my mother's eyes, and in a flash I knew what I had to say.

One day my dad surprised me with a brand new red bicycle, and then I realised it was my ninth birthday. The day I was selected to the Indian Institute of Technology, my parents arranged a party calling all my friends and theirs to celebrate. We were up until very late. I do not recall very well when people left. I had curled up and gone off to sleep on the sofa.

The train jerked and pulled to a stop. It was Gaziabad, another long hour to reach New Delhi. I looked at my wrist watch. It was nearly two in the morning. I was rudely dragged back to reality from my pleasant memories. My anxiety returned. The next was perhaps the longest hour of my life.

Vijay had come with Jayant to receive me at the New Delhi railway station. Vijay was Jayant's son, my age, studying economics in Delhi University. We had been close childhood friends. Jayant gave me a tight hug, but refused to answer my questions.

"We'll talk when we get home," he said.

From the tone of his voice and his face I knew that my worst fears had come true. We drove in silence. Once at home, Vijay took my bag away. Jayant took me to his study, asked me to sit down, and he went round the desk to take his seat. He explained to me that my parents were driving in the new Maruti along the ring road, when a lorry jumped red light and hit the car at speed on the driver's side. They had both died instantly. They were taken to casualty where my father was identified from papers he was carrying, and the university was informed. Their bodies were in the morgue, and will only be released the next day after post mortem.

I wanted to be alone for some time, and he left me, saying that some food and drink was left on the dining table, and I was to have it should I feel hungry. I had no tears in my eyes. My world had been ripped to pieces. Gradually the enormity of the situation was sinking in. I was alone in the world.

It took another twenty-four hours for the post mortem to be completed, and the bodies released. Jayant prevented me from going to the morgue. Eventually when I did see the shrouded bodies he advised me not to uncover them, and to remember my parents' faces as I last saw them, instead of the gruesome horror that I would otherwise encounter. The faces were badly disfigured in the accident. At the time I was numb my brain was not functioning and automatically did what I was told. I cremated the bodies and observed the Hindu religious rituals for ten days, and shaved my head. I scattered the ashes in the Yamuna River.

Jayant wanted me to stay with them until I got over my grief, and was able to go back to my engineering college. To me life had lost its meaning. I could not face living with my friends and relations. I knew the thought of my parents would haunt me every waking moment in familiar surroundings. I thought it was pointless studying engineering when my parents would not be able to applaud me on my success. For three days and nights I mulled over the problem of my future, and I decided that I needed a change of scenery to ease the intensity of my grief, to be able to rationalise. I wrote a long letter addressed to Jayant explaining my thoughts and my plan. I left the letter on the table in his study and walked out of the house after midnight carrying a small haversack. I went to the railway station, and boarded the first train available, going to Jammu. Somehow I slept through the journey and early next morning I found myself in Jammu railway station. I was hungry. Looking at my wallet I realised that I needed to start earning soon to be able to support myself.

I slung the haversack over my left shoulder and walked out of the station into the bright sunshine of a busy weekday. The town was already bustling with traffic and people going about their own businesses. Buses and Lorries were honking at errant rickshaw-pullers and push-carts that dared impede their progress. Cars were queuing behind. People and porters were entering the station to depart. I glided past the crowd onto the main road, and walked the pavement. It was a pleasant day. I tried to take some interest in my surroundings. The town was hemmed in on the North with high mountain ranges, extending to the East and West as far as I could see. A flat valley extended South wards helping the town to expand. There was no snow on top of the peaks near the town, but I could see some distant snow covered peaks glistening against the blue sky. The peaks close to town were probably of lesser height, and had dense vegetation of pine and fir and birch. Occasional rhododendron bushes, apple and apricot and cherry trees were in bloom creating flashes of colour against the green backdrop.

I walked slowly away from the centre and its noise and jostling crowd. I was passing what looked like an army cantonment with military barracks. I saw a banner advertising recruitment for the border roads. I had no idea what Border Roads was, but I needed a job. Without a second thought I joined the queue of young men under the banner. A man in his late fifties in a khaki uniform approached me and asked me if I wanted to join. He gave me a form to fill in. We were asked to sit a written examination comprising of a few simple questions on science and maths and general knowledge. A doctor checked us for any obvious disability and a short physical test was organised. I had no difficulty with any of those at all. Later I learnt that some of us have been selected for recruitment as pioneers in the Border Roads Organisation.

I went along with the flow and was issued with a pair of uniforms and ID badges. We had lunch, and the middle-aged man introduced himself as Shukra Oraon. He was an Assistant Engineer, and was supervising the recruitment. He told us that we would be on probation for six months, and then our jobs would be made permanent. We would have pension benefits. He explained that the Border Roads Organisation is responsible for building new roads and maintenance of existing roads in the hilly terrain of the sub Himalayan region and other parts of India. The organisation had to keep all strategic hilly roads open most of the year, clearing away snowdrifts and landslides. Our job would be to organise teams of manual labourers, and direct and supervise their activities. We were to get up early next morning, and were to be taken to Gulmarg, approximately a hundred and twenty-kilometre form Jammu, near Srinagar the state capital. Both army and civilian traffic use these roads, which were the only link the Himalayan state had with the rest of the country. We were to be part of 'Project Beacon'.

I had never been in a hilly terrain before. The majestic Himalayan ranges with snow flecked peaks, fast flowing streams with crystal clear water, thick pine forested landscape and the winding dual carriage-way taking us through dark tunnels and over gorges, hugging precipitous slopes, were all new to me. I was fascinated and excited. Small townships came and went—Katra, Udhampur, Baramulla—and then suddenly in front of us through a cleavage of two towering peaks we had our first glimpse of the valley of Srinagar, basking in the late afternoon sunshine, well below us. The Jhelum River appeared as a glistening ribbon flowing into the 'Dal Lake'. We gradually descended winding and twisting and hugging the slopes. The road was interspersed with sign postings like 'Be gentle on my curves' and 'Tiredness can kill' and 'Better late than never'.

That idyllic township next to the 'Dal' Lake was where most of the Bollywood romantic scenes were shot before producers and directors switched their attention to Switzerland, before the insurgency. Kashmir was once a very popular holiday destination for Indian and foreign tourists. Houseboats on the 'Dal' Lake were fully booked well in advance of the summer months.

We drove down the slope and skirting Srinagar, continued on our way to Gulmarg: another forty kilometres of picturesque landscape. We reached our destination just after Sunset and the near darkness of early tropical-evening saw us unlimbering our cramped muscles and stamping our feet to restore circulation. Our camp was next to a military cantonment, a short distance from the town. The ski slopes were pointed out to us. Of course at that time of the year there was no snow on the slopes. The whole place was blooming with wild flowers and orchids. Gulmarg certainly lives up to its name—'Road of flowers'. I had never imagined a place could be so enchanting, and so close to ones imagination of paradise. From Gulmarg, the higher peaks of the mighty Himalayas were more clearly visible, with their hauteur and majesty, covered in a mantle of snow—peering down at us, mere mortals. These timeless mountains can be quite intimidating at times, yet their attraction is irresistible. The purple sky was streaked with cirrus clouds. I was glad I came.

At this time of the year there was not much activity. The snow had melted, and our job mainly consisted of patching the potholes left behind. Our Road Construction Company was responsible mainly for maintenance of the roads from Baramulla to Gulmarg and beyond. My work consisted of driving up and down the road, identifying stretches in need of repair, especially to check for any weaknesses in the culverts and bridges needing buttressing and supports, and to look out for water logging and drainage problems. We often spent the night in the labour camps along the way. These were makeshift temporary camps, mostly tents and occasionally built of corrugated tin sheets, located near sites of work. Minor landslides were frequent following cloudbursts, and had to be cleared straight away. On the whole Shukra and I had ample free time, and spent a lot of time together. He treated me like his son. Though he guessed that I was well educated and had run away, except for occasional tactful remarks he never attempted to probe into my past.

On Sundays Shukra and I explored the trekking routes and mule tracks around Gulmarg. Summer in Gulmarg is beautiful, with carpets of wild flower covering gentle open slopes and meadows. Thickly forested pine scented conifers were surrounded by craggy snow capped barren peaks against a blue sky. Gurgling mountain streams rippling and dancing over rocks, shimmering in the golden dappled light under the green foliage. Where the water was deep, we could see shoals of trout gliding through crystal clear water against the white sandy bed of the stream. As the days slipped past, the pain and anguish of bereavement dulled. The loneliness I felt at loosing my parents became less intense. Their memory did not fade, but the loss became bearable. Shukra knew I was from a middle class family, but I could not bring myself to tell him about my past or the reasons for leaving home. We talked of nature, road conditions, the Border Road Organisation, and of places and people.

Shukra often spoke of his past, his experiences, and his achievements. He was born in a village in Chhotanagpur, a plateau in the present day Jharkhand State, and two thousand feet above sea level. His parents were poor. They did not own the land they farmed. The landowners and the farmers shared the crop equally. They lived in a thatched hut. The climate was pleasant in that forested land except in the monsoon, when for two months deluge of heavy torrential rain lashed the landscape, interspersed with thunder and lightening. This was the time when they planted paddy. Winter was fairly severe, with early morning frosts. Their village was surrounded by woodland consisting mainly of Sal and Banyan and Peeple trees, with occasional stands of Imli. There were thorny bushes of Babul, and Amla. Deer, fox and hyena were common, but sightings of cheetah or elephants were rare. A wide variety of birds nested in those trees. The hilly landscape with red mica strewn earth created gentle undulations and folds on the surface, hiding streams and lakes. Mountains in the plateau tended to be low and covered with lush vegetation.

The village life centred around a few huts near a lake which provided water for washing and bathing. A deep well was the source of drinking water. They had to physically lift water out of the well using a bucket and rope.

Shukra attended a catholic school near his village. He did not want to be a farmer, and had the wanderlust. At the age of sixteen he left home. He accompanied a man from his village to join the Border

Roads Organisation as a manual labourer in 'Project Hirak'. The town of Dhanbad, where the headquarters of the Project was located, was a four-hour bus journey away from his village. Rich coal mines surround Dhanbad. Border Roads Organisation had been tasked to create a road network around the mines to ease congestion and quick transportation of coal to the railhead. A few months later he became a 'pioneer' and was sent to 'Project Tusker' in the North East Frontier Area (NEFA), now Meghalay. The beauty of the land and the hospitality of the villagers enchanted him. He found that poverty was a common theme amongst all tribal people.

Shukra moved from 'Project' to 'Project', coal mines to Himalayan foothills, from the shores of Andaman Islands to the deserts of Libya, building new roads and bridges. In between he had visited his native village a few times, married a local girl when he was twenty-four, and became the proud father of a lusty boy. His nomadic life continued. His wife stayed back in the security of his village. He visited his family once or twice a year. His wife died of malaria when his son was nineteen.

His son joined the Indian Army, 2 Bihar infantry regiment. Shukra encouraged him to apply for selection to the Indian Military Academy, the only route open for other ranks to become an officer. He emerged as an officer after two years. From then on Shukra's contact with his son became less and less. His son married his Brigade Commander's daughter. Shukra visited his grand children once in a while. He found that the magnetism of the Himalayas was more alluring and the company of the men and women under him more attractive than the sophistication of army officers' wives and mess gossips. His son sometimes visited him, always alone. His wife did not show much enthusiasm for her father-in-law's company.

Winter was approaching. There was a nip in the air. Nights were colder, with hard frost in the mornings. Roads North of Gulmarg had closed. The Gujjars were coming down from the heights with their herd of goats and sheep. They camped on the banks of the Jhelum and other mountain rivers on their way to Mendhar and Naushera, warmer climate of lower altitudes. The ewes and the kids were carried by the men part of the way to protect them from the rigors of the trail. They would cross the Pir Panjal mountain ranges to reach Poonch and Rajouri and Mendhar. Once the snow started to melt, they would go back to the high plains. There are four passes through the Pir-Panjal ranges from Gulmarg to Poonch. The lowest one, Pir-Gali is at a height of eleven thousand feet and the highest—Chor-Panjal pass is at thirteen thousand and two hundred feet.

There had been a few inches of snowfall on the road from Srinagar to Gulmarg. We had kept all labourers and equipment on alert, in the event of a heavy fall. The roads had turned icy, and vehicles, both military and civilian, were using chains on wheels to prevent skids.

The weather was holding. On a bright Saturday morning Shukra and I decided to go for a trek up to the Chor-Panjal pass, camp the night and come back by Sunday afternoon. Work was under control. We carried our haversacks laden with tinned food, kerosene stove and an arctic tent.

We took to the trail. The slow climb along a mule track through pine forested land surrounded by snow-capped peaks under a clear sky looked ideal for such a trip. We had a short lunch break, and with light banter we enjoyed the walk up the gentle slope. Along the way small streams jumped and danced on rocks adjacent to the path, colourful birds would whisk past on spread wings from stooping over the dead field mouse it was about to peck or to catch the worm wriggling amongst the rocks. We did not see any animal, though we knew that the forest was teeming with them.

The weather decided to take a turn for the worse. Grey clouds started streaming across the sky, covering the sunshine we enjoyed all morning. The wind picked up and we felt the chill. Snow flakes floated down and across like puffs of cotton, gradually increasing in frequency and number, eventually becoming a flurry. We were covered in the white powder, and our noses were numb and watering, only to freeze over the bristles of our moustaches. Even through our mittens our fingers were picking up the chill. Earlier that afternoon we could see the saddle of the pass in the middle of serrated ridges and steep peaks, but now the world suddenly looked to be made of three shades—black and white and grey. We could no longer see the peaks. Even The tree-tops were hidden in the grey gloom and mist of low cumulus clouds and flying snow flakes. We looked for a flat surface under some trees to pitch our tent. It was nearly dark when we found a suitable spot.

We got into the tent, took off our parkas and lighted the stove. The tent was dry and warm. The wind could not find any chink to enter. We opened some tins, warmed the food over the stove, and ate till we were full. Our canteens were half empty by the time we finished our dinner. The wind howled outside, but in the tent we were snug and warm wriggling down into our sleeping bags. We switched off the stove, and picked up a pack of cards. We whiled away some time in torchlight, turned over and went to sleep.

Chirping of birds woke us up. I opened the tent flap and could not recognise the place. Wherever I ran my eye, the land and trees and rocks and bushes were all covered in snow. The white powder clung to everything. The Sun was just rising, but we were still in the shadows. Snow had banked on one side of the tent, pushing at its fabric. I walked up to the stream and washed my face, came back and woke Shukra up. We opened more tins and brewed hot tea for breakfast. We packed our haversack and started back. The snowdrift was much deeper than I expected. No track was visible. We followed the contour of the land. At places the snow was knee deep.

We realised that the moment we reached our base, we had to organise and mobilise working parties to clear the main road of snow. We trudged through the soft snow. I thanked Shukra for insisting that we wear our snow boots for this trek. Our progress was slow and painful. However, the scenery was beautiful, and sunny and calm. We worked up a healthy sweat despite the near freezing temperature.

We reached our base by dusk. On our way down the mountain we could gauge the scale of work awaiting us. It had been a heavy fall with drifts piling up to over fifteen feet in places. Shukra wanted to start work before the snow had a chance to harden into blocks of ice. I contacted the local contractors to supply us with more labourers than we had anticipated. I left instructions with group leaders at various labour camps to start shovelling the snow off the road. Once the tarmac was exposed, labour forces could leap-frog using lorries and gain valuable time. We were kept fairly busy for nearly a week to clean up the forty kilometres of the road. Work was labour intensive. This was my first chance at labour management on a big scale. Without Shukra's experienced help, I would have floundered, let alone achieve the efficiency and smoothness of operation for which I was commended.

Towards the end of the week snow was setting into hard blocks of ice, needing pickaxe to break it up. In the process, the tarmac was seriously damaged. The next two weeks were spent patching up the damage we did, blacktopping the surface and repairing culverts. We were working shifts almost round the clock. This road was strategically important for military and civilian population alike. This was the only road link for any kind of supply. In a real emergency air force helicopters had to be deployed to drop food and blankets in the remote villages, made inaccessible by snowdrifts. The local population is well aware of this perpetual problem. The elderly and the women with children came down to the towns to live with friends until the road is made accessible again. The fit and the young try to brave it out.

The army has no such choice. It has to man the pickets along the line of control with Pakistan all year round to stop infiltrators. In fact they organise patrols once every month along the line of control to look for evidence of infiltration, and seal up weak spots. Thousands of kilometres of winding ravines and deep gorges make it near impossible to stop infiltration, hence the need for manned pickets at every strategic location to hear or see unauthorised movement of men and animals through the inhospitable terrain.

Once in a while skirmishes do break out often with loss of lives. At other times spooked soldiers fire ammunition at shadows, escalating cross border exchange of fire, ranging from small arms to mortar and heavy artillery. Both sides are well entrenched behind concrete bunkers and soldiers rarely get hurt in these exchanges. It is the local villagers caught up in between who usually pay the price. Decades of attrition to the villagers have now become a way of life, a necessary hazard like mine blast injuries, and snake bites. The land around the line of control is heavily mined with anti personnel mines by both sides, and deadly vipers live in the tall grass covering the mountain slopes.

Over the ensuing days our friendship with the ski lodge caretakers paid off. I learnt to ski, and was tumbling or racing down empty slopes along with the instructor. Tourist season had not started. Only a few army officers and I monopolised the beautiful slopes around Gulmarg, needless to say, free of charge.

By late February tourists started to come. The volume of traffic on our roads increased many folds. I had to leave the slopes to monitor the road surface, look for landslides, divert water collections and visit labour camps to check on their welfare and distribute ration.

Sometimes our medical officer came along with me and held outdoor clinics and treated minor ailments. Serious patients were referred and transported to the district hospital in Srinagar.

Labour camps consisted of a huddle of tents and shacks built from corrugated metal sheets. Except for cooking ovens burning pinewood, there was no provision for heating water. Open-air toilets and trench latrines were customary. The brave bathed in the icy cold waters of the mountain streams—even when snowing.

We were more privileged, with a private temporary toilets and coal 'bukharis' (stoves) providing hot water and warmth in our temporary living quarters. Since the road works move from day to day over hundreds of kilometres, the workforce moved with it. All living accommodation was ad-hoc and temporary, hurriedly built and rapidly dismantled.

Eight months had passed since the day I left Jayant's house. The edge of my grief had blunted. I was taking more interest in my work and my surroundings. The out of the world natural beauty of Gulmarg and Shukra's companionship had helped me to overcome the tragedy that had befallen me, gave me the courage to face the world again.

I had written to Jayant, letting him know that I was well. I did not tell him my whereabouts or what I was doing. I had also informed the dean of my engineering college about the tragedy, and requested him to allow me to take some time out. I was hoping to save enough money to pay for my education. I was sure Jayant would have recovered some of my father's life insurance money from the insurance company on my behalf. I did not know how much life insurance cover my parents had. I did not care.

One evening when I came back from surveying the road to Sonamarg, Shukra informed me that he was transferred to another 'Project'—'Project Deepak'. There he would have to build new roads from Joshimath towards the border with China, at an approximate height of nine thousand feet. It will involve new cutting through rocks. The terrain was difficult, and they needed an experienced engineer to oversee the work. Shukra had arranged for my transfer as well, to accompany him to Joshimath. The new project was not due to start before July. There usually is only a window of three months before everything gets snowed under. We were not expected to leave before May. Shukra had to hand over to whoever was coming to replaced him. I had come to love Gulmarg, Sonemarg, and Tangdhar . . . . The beauty of Kashmir Valley was beyond words—pretty close to ones imagination of paradise.

Any change that is forced upon us causes some resentment, a reluctance to disrupt an established way of life. It also creates a flutter of excitement and anxiety at the prospect of visiting a new place—the challenge to tame nature in the wild, conform to new sets of people with their own foibles and idiosyncrasies and beliefs.

The news of our transfer appeared to have permeated to all our acquaintances. We started exchanging farewell greetings. We fell into our routine of checking the road surface, monitoring traffic and repairing damages. Most of our work was labour intensive. We did not have mechanised pavers. The tar had to be heated and mixed with stone chips by hand and shovelled manually onto the damaged road surface. The tar was spread evenly using rakes. We did have three heavy diesel rollers to stamp down and smooth the surface. We had one bulldozer, used to clear landslides. People from the workshop detachment were kept constantly busy nursing the old machinery and trying to keep them in a roadworthy and working order.

Time moved with amazing speed. Landscape changed. The black and white gave way to bursts of colour. Apple, cherry and apricot trees blossomed in shades of pink and white, showering the meadows and roads with their petals. To the uninitiated it appeared to be snowing on a bright spring morning. Wild flower shoots sprouted. Tender leaves started reappearing on the newly formed branches. Eventually by the time we had to leave, the valley was carpeted with flowers of various colours and shapes and sizes and height. Clear blue skies with occasional streaks of white cloud and golden sunshine replaced the blustery snowstorm. Faint breeze stirred the shrubs, creating the illusion that the flowers and the trees were bidding us au-ru-voir.

Shukra was silent and staring at the distance, wrapped in thought in his own world.

"Are you sad to leave this valley?" I asked, gently tapping him on his shoulder.

"No", he replied. "I was thinking about the last time I bade farewell to this Project. That was quite a few years ago. Then I was leaving behind four of my best mates, buried under tons of rocks in unmarked graves. All victims of accidental death while constructing the road to Chusul and Leh," he paused to swallow the lump in his throat. "I was in my early twenties then, almost your age," he continued. "I had no fear, and thought life was a big adventure. We had to take great risks, as time was at a premium and the weather most hostile."

"Will you tell me more about those days?" I asked.

"Project Beacon was established on 23 April 1960 with it's headquarter at Srinagar, and Brig. B P Wadhera was the Chief Engineer. A class five fair weather road existed from Srinagar to Kargil. In simple terms it means that the road could allow only one vehicle (jeep) at a time, and was a dirt track, that was impassable during wet weather or during the winter months. The road was treacherous in that it had a steep gradient. It had deep gorges on one side and the mountain slope on the other. There was very little room for error. Highest priority was accorded by the Indian Government to the construction of Srinagar-Leh road via Chusul, and the specifications had to be improved to a class nine all weather road. That means the road had to be a dual track black topped road, capable of sustaining traffic in all weather," Shukra started his narration.

"Why the sudden rush? Why was time at a premium?' I asked

"China had built roads up to its borders, and had improved telecommunication links. The Chinese were moving fast. With the annexation of Tibet and speedy development of communications right up to our traditional border, the ministers in Delhi feared that China was planning an attack and occupy Indian Territory. We had to build the infrastructure to support the logistics of impending war. We had to make sure that Lorries could travel as close to our borders as possible. It was imperative for troop movements and supplies. Roads were the only mode of transport available to the army"

"Please carry on," I urged.

"A four-pronged effort was launched to meet the deadline, braving the enormous logistics problem. Lt Col Puri's 5 Border Road Task Force was given sector Sonamarg to Kargil through the Zojilla pass. Though the Zojilla pass is at a height of 11,500 feet, up to forty feet of snow can accumulate on its surface and temperatures at night in winter can drop to minus forty degrees Celsius. Even today the major task every summer is to clear the Zojilla pass, which remains snow bound as late as June."

"9 BRTF was put on Kargil to Leh sector, and 6 BRTF started work on Leh to Chusul sector. 632 Corps Troops Engineers took on the Karu to Chusul road. Of the three passes along the road, Khardulgla was the highest at 18,380 feet followed by Thaglangla at 17,582 and then was Zojilla at 11,500. At the time of construction these were the highest motorable passes in the world. Anecdotes have it that if a convoy stopped even for ten minutes with running engine, the diesel in their tanks would freeze. This road went through Drass, the second coldest habitable place in the world."

"Baltal used to be a sleepy romantic village where India's first Prime Minister had spent his honeymoon. It became a bedlam of activity. Bulldozers and rock crushers plus all myriad of mechanical giants needed to build a road in this rocky region and beyond were to be heard throughout the day and night—a non stop cacophony of sound, matched only by the frenzied activity of the men."

"Baltal mirrored what was going on all along the two hundred and fifty two kilometres of the Srinagar-Leh road and beyond, to Chusul, via the Changla pass. The whole stretch was lashed unremittingly by blizzards, while unpredictable snowstorms tore at it with a suddenness that was awe-inspiring. Gumri was a freezing white world of snowfields, glaciers and icy winds. Landslides were frequent, and loss of machinery and men became a regular affair. Havaldar Sarwan Singh was of short stature. He escaped certain death from landslides three times. He was a cheerful sort of person with a sense of humour. He alleged that because of his small height, he managed to dodge the landslide and tumbling rock falls."

"Between the Suru and Waka Rivers is the 13,400 feet high Fatula, from where going down to the Indus River are the well known Hangroo loops of eighteen zigzag bends, dizzyingly descending 2,500 feet to the river. The first ever convoy of Lorries to negotiate the loops was on 29 May 1962. It was not without tragedy. The road covered with frozen snow, was as slippery as a sheet of greased glass and the vehicles were going at a snails pace to avoid skidding. No sooner had the first vehicle negotiated the turn, there came from somewhere, an earth-shattering sound. Other vehicles screeched to a halt, and we got down. To our stunned horror we saw the first vehicle bouncing down the embankment like a rubber ball. It stopped on its hood 400 feet below us. It was a sight I shall never forget."

We reached Srinagar by evening. We stayed the night at the Task Force headquarter, and caught the earliest bus next morning for Jammu, the nearest railhead. In the bus Shukra told me that he had been promoted to Superintendent Engineer, and was going as OC of a Road Construction Company under 21 BRTF. I was pleased for him, for his years of struggle and hard work has brought him some reward. I congratulated him. He has been asked to oversee a new road construction near Badrinath in 'Project Deepak'. He tried to persuade me to go back home. I did not tell him that I had no home. I was not yet ready to go back to familiar surroundings. The Dean of my Engineering College had permitted me to take a year out, and I had a few more months.

I asked Shukra to explain to me why the Border Roads Organisation was created and what it does. I wanted to know how big and varied this organisation was. Shukra tried, in his own words and using his own interpretation of events, to explain:

"Border Roads was born to fill in a void, a necessity in the development of independent India. Once India became a Sovereign Democratic Republic, the senior politicians and bureaucrats felt that there was no effective means of communication with the hilly districts in the Himalayan foothills, stretching for over two thousand

and five hundred kilometres: From Kargil to Kohima, from Laddakh to Mezoram, from the desolate mountainous Afghanistan border to the thickly forested Burmese border, from the Corbett national park in the Garhwal district to Sikkim. There was an urgent need to bring all tribal communities into the mainstream of India for integration and security of the borders of the country."

"In 1959, after assessing the tasks and inherent problems the Engineer in Chief (Army) suggested a five year construction programme for our borders. Creation of a new organisation was envisaged. Meanwhile the situation on the borders suddenly worsened, and a major clash appeared imminent. The time frame of five years was telescoped to two years. A committee of Secretaries examined the entire case. Since the difficult terrain and time were two major considerations besides resource mobilisation, it was felt that contracts and decisions must be vested with a body whose functioning could not be hindered by the procedural difficulties or independent actions at State level. Accordingly in February 1960, the union Cabinet decided to set up the Border Roads Development Board (BRDB) under the chairmanship of the Prime Minister. The defence minister was made the deputy chairman."

"Addressing the first meeting, Prime Minister J L Nehru emphasised that Laddakh and North Eastern Frontier Area (NEFA) deserved the highest priority. Gen. K S Thimayya pointed out the importance of early construction of Leh-Kargil road because that had to be the basis of construction of further roads forward of that area. Air lifting of plant, machinery and construction material for this road was essential. He placed equal importance on Chardaur—Tawang road in NEFA. The then Chief of Air Staff, Air Marshall S Mukherjee pointed out the need for bigger transport aircraft and helicopters to meet the demand. Thus an independent organisation for construction of border roads with immediate tasks was born."

"An unprecedented organisational whirl was set in motion immediately after the first meeting. Works in Laddakh and NEFA were to commence immediately and in Sikkim later that year. For the execution of the projects departmentally, the World War II concept of General Reserve Engineer Force (GREF) was once again revived. This was to be largely a civilian organisation with a happy blend of personnel from Army. It was structured on Army pattern for command and control, logistics and administration. The personnel were found both from Army and civil services including deputationists from central and state government bodies."

"GREF Centres at Roorkee and Allahabad were speedily raised for the training of new recruits and allotment of trades. By May 1960, ten Task Forces were in the process of being raised, some largely by amalgamation and restructuring of Corps of Engineers units and others recruiting a predominance of ex-servicemen to the tune of seventy per cent."

"The second meeting of the BRDB was held on 12 May 1960 where 01 Jun 1960 was decided as the target date for commencement of work by the organisation. The Border Roads Organisation was to take over roads in more forward and comparatively difficult terrain. As per the initial estimate, the entire plan was to be completed by the end of 1962. Roads were to conform to fair weather class five (single lane) or class 9 (double lane) specifications. Total length of roads planned was four thousand seven hundred and eighty five miles covering Jammu and Kashmir, Assam, Sikkim, NEFA (now Arunachal Pradesh), Punjab, Himachal Pradesh and Uttar Pradesh. Nearly forty five per cent of these roads were entirely to be new construction and the rest involved the development of the existing tracks. Until late fifties, communications in border areas were virtually non-existent. In J&K, Leh was connected with Srinagar by road fit only for light transport vehicles, that too for four months (Jul-Oct) in a year. In Punjab and Himachal, the transport could ply only up to Rahala—at the foot of the Rohtang pass; while on the Hindustan-Tibet road nothing existed one hundred miles beyond Simla. Sikkim had no motor able road beyond Gangtok, except jeep track to Nathula. In NEFA, only fair weather jeep tracks existed up to Bomdila and Zero. In the Mizo hills, the mule tracks were being gradually widened to take the jeeps. In the interior of Nagaland, only three-ton trucks with four-wheel-drive could be trusted to move. Even the rear links were in an extremely poor and unreliable shape." Shukra stopped his narration, and looked out of the window.

Our bus was approaching Jammu. The National-Highway from Srinagar to Jammu is a dual carriageway, passing through Anantpur, Baramullah, Udhampur and Katra, and through a long tunnel. Traffic was fairly heavy. It was late afternoon, and our train to New Delhi was scheduled to leave at nine O'clock in the evening, for an overnight journey reaching its destination at six in the morning.

JOSHIMATH

We stretched our legs in the crowded narrow streets of Jammu's main market, absorbing the bustling activity around us. The mingled aroma of spices, fish and rotting vegetables, the jostling of the ever moving stream of humanity, the ear-splitting noise of traffic and hawkers made me realise that I had been away from city life too long. I loved the atmosphere; I felt alive.

When it grew dark, we had dinner in a restaurant and made our way to the railway station. The train was on schedule. We had a berth each. We slept. An uneventful ride saw us in New Delhi the next morning. We took a taxi to the Interstate Bus Terminal. The next leg of the journey involved a bus ride to Hrishikesh. Shukra expected a Task Force jeep to meet us at Hrishikesh to drive us up into the heart of Garhwal (Uttarakhand) and to Joshimath. Since it would be late afternoon by the time we reach Hrishikesh, we planned to stay the night there and start for Joshimath the next morning, another six hours drive through winding climbing picturesque mountain roads.

Hrishikesh is a pleasant small town at the Himalayan foothills. From here the road starts winding up, snaking around mountain ranges, skirting gorges, straddling bridges, bypassing towns, villages and hamlets, meandering along the contours of the land to climb higher and higher into the lap of the Himalayas. Though this part of the country was new to me, Shukra had worked on these roads before.

We sat on the bank of the fast flowing Ganges, where it leaves the mountains to enter the great Indo-Gangetic plain, the rice bowl that feeds the billion Indians. This life-giving river is considered to be holy, and is held sacred by the Hindus. The Sun was loosing its glare as it progressed on its Westerly path. We had nothing to do, with time to kill. I was chucking pebbles into the river, and watched the ripples being swept away even before they could form. I was speculating on what lay ahead and what should my future be.

We were to stay the next evening at Pipli, a platoon headquarter near Joshimath. The Assistant Engineer in charge of that platoon was Shukra's old friend, and had requested that we spend the evening with him. It had been a few years since Shukra had last met him, and was looking forward to an evening of reminiscence.

Hrishikesh to Joshimath is a winding single carriageway; wide enough to allow long private buses to compete for the fare of pilgrims and tourists to the various attractions that hide in the folds of the mountain ranges. Badrinath, a Hindu pilgrimage is located a few miles beyond Joshimath. The famous temple there stays closed and snow bound for six months every year. Ceremonious openings of the doors take place every May. There are a few pilgrimages beyond Badrinath, places where mule tracks are the only access. Some of the other places are only accessible by walking over glaciers. Faith brings many old and infirm to these parts and gives them the strength to complete their quest. Pilgrims usually travel in small groups and trek the trails to their objectives. The roads get fairly busy during the summer months as pilgrims and tourists from all over India and beyond come here.

I learnt later that there are many other places of interest in these hills. I did not know at the time how familiar these places would become, and how these places would enrich my life.

On our way to Joshimath we followed the River Ganges toward its origin. As we climbed higher and higher, the river became narrower and swifter, creating white water rapids at places. The gorges also became steeper and deeper, at places becoming sheer cliffs a couple of thousand feet from the river bed.

Prayag means confluence of two or more rivers, and on our way we crossed many prayags like Karna Prayag, Dev Prayag, Rudra Prayag and Bishnu Prayag. These are the various points where large mountain streams join the main river. At Rudra Prayag River Mandakini joins Alaknanda, and at Dev Prayag two streams of equal importance—Bhagirathi and Alaknanda meet to form The Ganges.

Legends say that a prince named Bhagirath went up to the Himalayas and worshipped Shiva. Pleased with him, Shiva granted him his wish to bring Ganges to Earth from the Heavens. Apparently River Ganges followed Bhagirath down the slopes of the Himalayas, through the Indo-Gangetic plain to merge into the Bay of Bengal. Thus the main stream of Ganges that originates from the Gomukh glacier and run through Gangotri and Uttarkashi is called Bhagirathi, until it meets Alaknanda at Dev Prayag.

A large painting of a Royal Bengal Tiger attracts the eye at Rudra Prayag where the road makes a sharp bend as it climbs the slope. This painting is to remind visitors that this forested land forms part of Jim Corbett national park, a tiger reserve. This forest was haunted by the 'Man eater' depicted in the picture, killing many villagers and immortalised by Jim Corbett in his book "The Man eaters of

Kumaon". Once tigers reigned supreme in these forests but now have dwindled to near extinction.

We stayed the night at Pipli as planned. Shukra's friend told us that a number of labourers have been recruited for our new project, and that they were staying in a temporary camp near by. Shukra had stayed up late with his friend reminiscing and catching up. I had left them just after dinner, and had gone to bed early. I woke up before Sunrise the next morning, and decided to go for a jog. The sky was getting brighter. Through the trees I glimpsed reflections on water. I was surprised to see a lake at this height, and in a place with narrow gorges. I stepped off the road, and slid down the slope towards the edge of the water—and stopped. I saw a beautiful silhouette, a young woman stood waist deep in water. She was taking dips in the icy water. Obviously she wanted to bathe in privacy and seclusion. I sat down on a rock observing, in silence. I did not want to surprise or embarrass her. I also wanted to savour the beauty of the moment. She eventually came out of the water, the rays of the early Sun glistening over her wet naked body. She dried herself leisurely savouring the tranquillity and beauty of the nascent morning, oblivious of her admirer, bending forward to shake out her long dark hair and squeezing the water out of the locks. She put on her sari and walked off in the opposite direction with a wistful backward glance at the lake, not realising that she was under observation. I went up to the road and resumed jogging back. I wondered who she was, probably a local villager. Somehow I found myself thinking of her, and feeling a bit sad that I was not going to see her again. Later that day, after reporting to BRTF Headquarters we were supposed to locate a suitable camp in our new work site. The labourers were to join us within a week, when work would start in earnest.

I had always been good at studies and sports, consequently people at my school or college seemed to know me by my name and I rarely had to introduce myself. I think girls in my college were interested and curious about me, but they did not attract me beyond the casual relationship of fellow students. I was too engrossed with my studies and training and hobbies to have much free time. Somehow this girl was different. I did not see her at close quarters, yet I felt an attraction towards her that was alien to me. I wished I had walked up to her. I wondered what language she spoke. My knowledge of the local dialect was very limited. I realised that I have to improve my language skills to give meaningful instructions to the labourers under me, if I were to achieve desired results.

I was so immersed in my thoughts, a silhouette of immense beauty filling my conscious mind, that my legs automatically continued their rhythmic motions and I almost ran past our camp. I retraced my steps. Fortunately the road was devoid of traffic at that time of the morning. I filled up two buckets with cold water from the stream, and headed for the make shift toilet for a wash.

The road head to the site of new cutting was only ten kilometres from Joshimath, towards Badrinath Dham. The actual rock face could be reached driving over a twenty five kilometre stretch of dirt track. Our objective that summer was to carve out a ten kilometre length of new road towards the Indo-Tibetan-Chinese border. The strategists had decided to have parallel roads at frequent intervals going up to the border from the main Hrishikesh-Joshimath-Badrinath road. We had until early October not only to finish cutting and blacktopping the new road, but also widening improving and blacktopping the existing dirt track.

Shukra and I did a few reconnaissance trips to the rock face. Army surveyors and engineers had already planned the formation cutting and tunnels, and the Task Force had recruited and allotted the required labour force and machinery for the work to our Road

Construction Company. We were to get fifty men and women, one bulldozer, a stone crusher, a generator, a field telephone, a lorry and one jeep. Some tents and blankets were also sanctioned. The supply vehicle would visit us once a week and the workshop team every fortnight for vehicle maintenance, unless we desperately needed them. We had a tight schedule. We laid cables for the field telephone, connecting us to the BRTF Headquarter.

Shukra decided to widen and blacktop the existing track first, to facilitate easy access for the second phase of the operation. There was another reason. We were new to this labour force. Shukra thought routine work would help to familiarise ourselves, and also give him an idea of their experience in road works. Once a trust and rapport builds up riskier tasks would be easy to delegate. For the first phase of the work, Shukra decided that the labour camp should be located five kilometres down the dirt track. He ordered equal quantities of bitumen drums and stone chips to be placed every kilometre of the way. The first task was to widen the track. Shukra was quite keen to know the labourers individually, and get their trust. To this end he decided to stay close to their camp site.

The first few kilometres of the road was easy to widen, as it ran along a mountain stream through forested land. Except for a gradient of one in ten, the construction work was fairly straight forward. The labour force was split up into two groups. Shukra supervised one group working towards the main road, and I took the other group working away from the main road starting from the camp site. We cut trees, moved rocks, levelled soil and filled depressions. We fed the big rocks to the crusher, and used the small stones to fill holes, stomping and firming them in place. We used rakes to even out the surface, and checked the gradient with spirit levels. Once satisfied the heavy roller was used to prepare the surface for blacktopping. There was easy camaraderie, helped by uncomplicated work and good weather.

We worked six days a week, Sun up to Sun down. The camp woke up early and after a hot breakfast the group walked to their work stations, carrying shovels, spades, pickaxe and crow-bars with them. Two were left behind to cook a simple lunch, and a more appetising dinner for all.

Our camp consisted of twenty tents, sleeping four in most. Shukra and I shared a tent. We had a storage tent containing our ration, and another containing tools and spare blankets. Two of the tents were pitched a couple of hundred metres away from the main camp, and housed explosives and diesel, petrol and kerosene. Though we were in a remote place, and ten kilometres from the nearest village, Shukra posted two guards every night. Guards were not necessary during the day as the approach road in either direction would be humming with people and activity. Also, the tents were in plain sight of the camp, and the cooks could keep an eye.

As in all such temporary camps, we had erected make shift toilets, and deep trench latrines were dug up a few hundred metres from the camp for different sexes. The wooden platform and canvas screens were purpose built, and was supplied through the army. One of the tasks on Sundays was to fill up the trenches, and relocate the latrines. The medical team visited us every Sunday and tended to problems if any. Mostly it took the form of minor burns and infections, common cold or diarrhoea. Occasionally patients requiring closer observation were taken to the Task Force Headquarter, to return when fully fit. The labourers were paid on a daily basis, and no sick leave was allowed, hence no one reported sick unless forced to by ill health or injury.

Gradually I fell into an easy rhythm. Get up in the morning, have breakfast, allocate work, supervise smooth functioning, break for lunch, resume work and then trudge back to the camp, wash, eat, chat around the camp fires and eventually hit the bed.

This phase of the work was not demanding, and work progressed at a fast pace. Once the surface was prepared for blacktopping, stones were laid and impacted with the heavy roller. The bitumen was heated on stretched empty bitumen drums made into sheets and mixed with stone chips manually using shovels. Once thorough mixing was ensured, the mixture was shovelled on the road surface, and clumps were evened out using rakes. A six inch thick layer of tar and stone mixture was then impacted in place by the heavy roller again. The surface was checked for gradient, and a gentle slope from the centre outward was left for run off of rain water from the road surface. Shallow trenches on either side of the road edge facilitated the process. The last thing we wanted was the rain water getting under the surface, and washing away the soil, cracking the surface and leaving pot-holes. We did five hundred metres at a time. We used fire wood from the forest to melt the tar and heat the mixture. Since laying and paving were done manually the work was labour intensive and slow.

In the evenings I would sit with Shukra after dinner and discuss the work at hand. He seemed satisfied with the progress. Though it was summer, because of the altitude, a chill crept in the air after Sunset. We were in a clearing and the tents were pitched in a semi-circle, leaving a central grassy embankment gently sloping towards the stream. A few fires would spring up exaggerating the gloom. This was the time of the day when we could relax and socialise, and get to know each other. The tired muscles soaked up the heat from the fire and lethargy of contentment spread through the body. Rarely heated arguments broke out and Shukra would walk up to the recalcitrant parties and smooth their ruffled feathers. On the whole there was harmony and understanding in the camp.

I stopped speaking in mid sentence as a melodious voice floated across the camp. A popular haunting Hindi song beautifully rendered. I turned my head to locate the voice and noticed everyone was craning their heads.

"Who's singing?" I asked Shukra.

"I don't know." He replied. "Let's go and find out."

We walked towards the fire around which a group of women were sitting and one of them was singing. As we came closer, I saw her. I felt the same attraction and an exultation at seeing her again. She saw us coming and stopped.

"No, please don't stop. We have come to listen to you." Shukra said, and sat down outside the circle. They shifted to make room to include us into the circle. She was embarrassed, and the firelight playing on her face prevented her from being able to hide her emotions. She looked down and was playing with an errant strand of hair that had escaped the restraint of her hair band. Shyly she looked up at us, and seeing nods of reassurance from Shukra, took up where she had left. I was entranced. She had a lovely voice, and the location, the situation, the atmosphere and the unexpectedness created a spell, an out of the world feeling. Others gradually drifted over in ones and twos, until almost the whole camp surrounded her.

After a few songs she said, "Would anyone else like to sing now please, this party is getting very one sided."

After initial protests, Ashwini, our bulldozer operator took up the challenge. With the ice broken, scattered voices picked up the tempo, and I found myself joining in the chorus. Shukra broke up the party saying it was getting late, and we had work to do next morning.

I learnt her name was Rini, and she worked as a labourer in Shukra's group. She looked very young. I felt like asking Shukra to swap groups, and then realised that would be silly. I'll have to get work out of her, and couldn't just stare at her or monopolise her in front of twenty five others!

Over the next few days we had singing and performances around the campfire. I found no opportunity to isolate her from her entourage without raising eyebrows. It appeared that the other women were very protective towards her.

One morning I was brushing my teeth by the stream, when I heard a scream. I ran towards the sound, and initially did not see anyone. I heard a shout again, and then looked closely to find Rini's face peeping over the edge of the cliff. She was walking along the cliff edge, looking at the fast flowing river below when suddenly the ground crumpled and gave way under her weight. Fortunately there was a wide ledge beyond the rim and she fell on it. She was not hurt, but scared. I pulled her up. She was shaking. I held her and tried to calm her down. I took her away from the edge. When she was sufficiently recovered, we went back to the camp. I informed Shukra about the incident, and he circulated a message asking everyone not to go far from the camp alone. That evening when we gathered around the camp fire, she gave me a weak smile. After the group dispersed looking for bed, I stayed back and she appeared to want to talk to me. She thanked me. It was my turn to be at a loss for words. I do not remember what I said, but we stayed up quite late. From that night on it developed into a routine that after everyone left, we would be talking for sometime, getting to know each other. Others acknowledged this tacit arrangement, and did not disturb us. Rini told me about her childhood and her upbringing. In turn I confided in her. Once or twice Shukra had a dig at me, but when he realised that I was serious, he stopped teasing me. He reminded me that she was very young, and that I should think carefully before committing myself.

We had been working for two months, and had completed twenty miles of resurfaced road. It was mid July. I asked Shukra if I could take Rini to visit some of the local attractions. We would leave on Saturdays in the late afternoon, and be back by Sunday evenings. Shukra had no objections. His only stipulation was to make sure that I was at work on time on Monday mornings. We were five kilometres away from the rock face where the second phase of the work was to begin, Work was on schedule. I decided to go to the 'Valley of Flowers' first, and Shukra agreed to drop us off at Govind Ghat, five kilometres from the road head.

I was quite excited. I gathered from the locals that there is a mule track from Govind Ghat to the village of Ghangriyan, a distance of seventeen kilometres and a climb of five thousand feet to ten thousand feet above the sea level. We carried a small satchel each with a spare set of clothes and toiletteries. Rini was quite fit, and we set off at a brisk pace. The last thing we wanted was to get lost in the gathering gloom of late evening. It turned out that our fears were unfounded, as the track was well worn, and dotted with wayside shops and restaurants offering limited wholesome fare.

I was an only child, and all my life I was carefree, occasionally even thoughtless regarding others' needs and comforts. On that day suddenly I realised that I was responsible for Rini, and I did care. We walked through a canopy of foliage. Birch, Spruce and Pine dotted the forest lining the track, allowing very little Sunlight at that time of the evening. We could see the cloudless sky through gaps in the foliage change colour from blue to crimson, pink and then a purplish grey hue, merging unnoticed into the night. The walk was invigorating, stimulating a healthy appetite. We held hands most of the way, talking and laughing and listening. I felt a happiness and contentment I had never experienced before.

There were undergrowths of rhododendron bushes in bloom. A sweet fragrance from other nameless plants and orchids enveloped us. One by one the stars appeared on the darkening sky. A gentle moonlight bathed the village as we reached Ghangriyan.

We went to 'Guru ka Langar', a charitable institution run by the Sikh Gurdwara committee, providing free food and lodging to all comers. They gave us a couple of blankets each. After dinner, we headed for separate dormitories. The male dormitory was half full, and locating an empty corner I spread one of the blankets on the floor, and wrapped the other around me. In no time I was fast asleep. Early morning chill woke me up. I folded my blankets and returned them. As I was up almost before dawn, there was no queue for the toilet. I washed myself in the cold water. The light became brighter, with Sunlight hitting the mountain peaks. Since the village was surrounded by tall peaks, we were still in shadows.

There are two tracks from Ghangriyan. One leads to the "Valley of Flowers", and the other, a much steeper track, leads to "Hemkunt Sahib", a Sikh pilgrimage, at fifteen thousand feet. Many visitors come only to visit the "Hemkunt Sahib", and probably do not know of the existence of the Valley of Flowers. It is said that Guru Nanak, the first Sikh Guru had come to Hemkunt for meditation, and this place of pilgrimage is second in the scale of reverence to the Sikhs only to the Golden Temple at Amritsar.

I could see many elderly Sikhs with their wives starting to embark on the arduous second phase of the climb. The track to the Valley of Flowers, on the other hand is a gentle slope, climbing only a thousand feet over a distance of four miles.

We had breakfast. Rini was looking beautiful. I wanted to hug and kiss her, but that is not in keeping with the Indian traditions, and would raise a lot of eyebrows in this pilgrim infested village. I restrained myself, and contented with holding her hand. We giggled like children and set off for the Valley. The track was lined with the ubiquitous Birch and Spruce and Pine and Rhododendrons bushes. Other wild flowers had also tried to exist resisting the monopoly, splashing the wayside with streaks of colours of various shades.

Once the track took a bend, hiding us from the village and its population, I embraced Rini, and planted a gentle lingering kiss on her lips. She must have liked it, for she responded at first, and then pushed me away, admonishing me and hurrying me towards our objective. I laughed and followed her.

We entered the mouth of the valley and stood spell bound. I had not imagined even in my wildest dreams the splendour that lay in front of us. Bathed in early morning sunshine was probably the largest garden in the world: eighty seven hectares of the valley floor was carpeted with more than two hundred and fifty species of flowers, orchids and lilies. This valley is part of a glacial corridor eight miles long and two miles wide, watered by the Pushpawati River, that originates here and then tumbles down to join the Mandakini River beyond the valley. There are many streams crisscrossing the valley. The small ones can be waded across but the wider ones have log crossings or glacial bridges across them. There is only one paved track through the valley. Anyone wishing to deviate from the track will have to wade through knee deep flowers, crushing some of them in the process. It is said that the Gods had showered flowers into this valley. Folklore has it that this is the playground of the fairies, and anyone venturing deep into the valley is waylaid, and lost for ever. Others say there are flowers with such strong fragrance, that people who smell it, faint.

Though the local shepherds have been grazing their cattle in this valley since ancient times, the valley was introduced to the world by Frank S Smyth, explorer and botanist. After a successful expedition to conquer mount Kamet, on the return journey he was lost, and stumbled into this valley in 1931. He again came back to this valley in 1937, and wrote a book "The Valley of Flowers". In 1939, Kew Gardens in London sent Miss Joan Margaret Leggie to study the plants here. Unfortunately, while collecting plants from mountain slopes, she fell to her death. Her sister erected a tombstone where locals had buried her, and etched on the marble are the words:

"I will lift up mine eyes
Unto the Hills
From whence cometh my strength."

Rini was beside herself with excitement. She flitted from flower to flower like the bees and the butterflies that hovered and darted and buzzed around us. We saw geraniums, flox, wild roses, delphiniums, forget-me-nots, primula, dianthus, petunia, ranenculi, edelweiss, Himalayan blue poppy, and the rare Bramh-Kamal and scores more of unknown variety of flowers of shapes and sizes and colours beyond imagination. One flower looked exactly like the head of the venomous cobra. We explored the valley, lay on the flowers, drank from the crystal clear icy cold streams and ran around sang songs and exhausted with emotional upheaval sat on a vantage point, drinking in the beauty with our eyes, etching it in our memory for posterity and holding each other to reassure us that we were not dreaming.

Hunger brought us back to the real world. Reluctantly we dragged our feet towards the village, frequently looking back. We were subdued on our way back, especially after seeing the grave. We were filled with a serenity I had not known before, squashing all other emotions.

After lunch we decided to go up the other track to Hemkunt Sahib as well, a six kilometre trek, but climbing another five thousand feet. We were stopping every couple of hundred metres to catch our breath. The thin air made breathing laborious. Two soldiers from the

Sikh Light Infantry ran past us. We looked at each other, raised our eyebrows and rolled our eyes and grinned at each other.

"They must be posted in a high altitude area," I said.

Rini was too busy breathing hard, and did not bother to reply. An American girl, with a haversack on her back was panting in front of us. We overtook her. She smiled at us and we reciprocated.

Eventually we reached the top. We were unprepared for the huge 'Gurdwara' building standing next to a lake. To build at this height of fifteen thousand feet above sea level speaks volumes of man's endurance and determination. The lake was fed by melting snow from the surrounding peaks. We saw many elderly Sikhs taking a dip in the lake before entering the Gurdwara. Keeping in mind that we had to return to our camp that night, we had a quick look inside the Gurdwara, and took to the tracks.

Descent was easier and quicker. From Hemkunt Sahib to Govind Ghat, a descent of ten thousand feet and twenty three kilometres, took us a little over four hours. We walked back to our camp after having dinner at Govind Ghat. By the time we reached camp, it was fairly late, and most people were fast asleep. Shukra was waiting for us. He had kept some food warm for us. We ate what we could, thanked him and went to bed.

Next day it was work as usual. In the evening around the campfire I was describing to Shukra what we saw. He smiled at us and said, "I have been there many times in the past. It is a lovely place, a place to forget oneself and also a place to discover"

I thought I understood what he meant by those words.

"I hear there is a plan to divert Pushpawati River's flow through a tunnel to augment upper Alaknanda for a hydroelectric project.

If it goes through, the Valley of Flowers may dry up and kill all the flowers," He added. "The government engineers and ecologists are looking into it."

I kept quiet. The thought of the valley without the flowers was too ghastly to contemplate.

"Doctor came this morning and took Thapa with him. He has been admitted to the District Hospital," Shukra said changing the subject. "I believe he has anaemia from Malaria, and needs blood transfusion. Due to lack of blood, his heart is not pumping well, and is getting bigger."

Thapa was a nineteen year old labourer. When he joined us, he was very active and enthusiastic. However over the past couple of weeks, he was feeling very weak, and was easily getting out of breath. He was also running a high temperature on alternate days, with chills and shaking.

"I have suspended work for tomorrow," Shukra continued. "I would like some of you to go to the hospital tomorrow, and give your blood samples. They will check your blood groups, and cross match your blood with Thapa's to see whose blood will be suitable for him; then you can decide to donate your blood."

Around twenty of us boarded the lorry and went to Joshimath. We were asked to wait in a queue. Blood samples were taken from us and cross-matched with Thapa's blood. Five of us with blood group O positive were selected. After giving blood, we went to see Thapa in the ward. He greeted us with a weak smile. He looked really pale and weak. Any exertion caused him to breathe hard. The doctor in charge of ward told us that he will be alright after blood transfusion, and being a young person, should make a full recovery. We prayed for him. A subdued group returned to the camp that evening, and no one lingered at the campfire. I spent some time with Rini after dinner, and then went back to my tent.

The road works was going to plan. Everything had settled into a routine, and we were almost at the rock face. The nearer we approached the rock face, the more serious Shukra became. He told me that controlled blasting of the rock face in the Himalayas always had the risk of landslides. He would much prefer to work with granite, or older mountains, though it would be slower work. He had planned to set off the charges in the late afternoon, and withdraw a couple of miles to the campsite for the night. Next morning the labour force would go and clear the debris, break up loose rocks with pickaxes, and create a twenty feet wide ledge. He had requested BRTF Headquarter to attach a couple of masons to his company, to make the culverts and buttresses to stabilise the mountainside. In places where the slope of the mountain was steep, he planned to cut through, leaving an overhang, and support it with concrete pillars. It would to be hazardous work, and he was instructing everyone, including me, about safety regulations which had to be followed strictly.

Very early that Sunday morning Shukra dropped Rini and me at Badrinath, ten miles from our road head, and a good thirty kilometres from our present camp location. Badrinath is an ancient Hindu pilgrimage. Though the present temple was built by the Garhwal kings a couple of centuries ago, the original temple is supposed to have been there for over six thousand and five hundred years. Devotees from all over India come here. This temple opens in May and is closed in October, amidst much fanfare and festivities. It remains snowed under during the winter months. There are many hotels and dormitories and charitable institutions around the place to accommodate bus loads of visitors. Legends and mythology is deeply intertwined with this place of worship. There is a hot water lake near the temple. The water temperature remains at fifty five degrees Celsius, even though the ambient temperature drops well below zero in the winter. Devotees bathe in the lake before entering the temple. The water of the lake is credited with having medicinal values. The temple has a high decorative façade, with three large chambers. Devotees congregate in the outer chamber, while the idol is kept and worshipped in the middle chamber.

A three kilometre walk from the temple took us to Vyaas Caves. Inside one of these caves, there are rock formations that resemble, and appear to be piles of ancient manuscripts, written on barks of birch tree. 'Bhurja Patra', as it is known was probably the first material used for writing manuscripts, much before papyrus. It is alleged that a Vedic Sage, Vyaas compiled the Vedas into four groups. The oldest, Rig Veda is thought to be ten thousand years old. He had also compiled other works like the Puranas, and the Indian epic Mahabharata.

We looked around in awe. The legends and the time span were beyond imagination. The confines of the cave overwhelmed me in other ways. I put my hand on Rini's shoulders, and asked her, "Will you marry me?"

"What, Now!" She said jokingly.

I smiled and embraced and kissed her before she could say any more.

"No" I said, "I'll have to go back to my college and complete my engineering degree. I want to get a proper job first. I have spoken to Shukra about it, and he said that he would be honoured if you agreed to stay with him. He referred to you as the daughter he always wished for but never had. He will be retiring soon, and plans to settle down in Shimla."

"What am I supposed to do in the meantime? How often am I going to see you?" Rini asked.

"Well, I'll visit you during the holidays, and shall write to you often. When Shukra gets a phone, we can talk often. As for what you will do depends on whether you want to continue with formal education or learn music, or both."

Rini did not answer. She put her arms around my shoulders and held me tightly, putting her head on my chest. I tilted her chin up, and realised that she was crying.

"I never had anything or anyone I could call my own." She stammered, "Whenever I got fond of anyone or anything or any place, I lost it for ever. I lost my mother, I had to leave the orphanage; I had to leave my friends. I am scared that I may loose you as well," she pleaded with tearful eyes.

"Nonsense," I said, "Lets go, its time to head back for the camp."

Wrapping my right arm around her waist I guided her out of the gloomy cave into the bright afternoon.

We were walking back to the camp, and half way down the road we met Shukra in his jeep, coming to fetch us. He picked us up, and drove us back rest of the way. We were so quiet in the car, that Shukra was forced to ask if we had quarrelled, producing a gurgle of merriment and spontaneous laughter from Rini.

Later that evening I told Shukra what happened, and my future plans. I had already asked him if he would keep an eye on Rini for me until

I am ready to take the responsibility, and he had been more than happy to oblige. He had told me that he was going to do that anyway. He said that he had an ulterior motive. He wanted to hear her sing, and he wanted some company when he retired. He did not want to be bored out of his mind. He congratulated me and shook my hand. I was moved to protest that she had not said 'yes' yet.

Somehow everyone in the camp seemed to know that we were engaged. I was greeted with broad smiles and congratulatory salutations. I must admit that I was a bit euphoric myself. I could not concentrate on the work at hand, and often caught myself thinking of going over to Shukra's group. It was fortunate that the days work involved routine activity, and there was no need to keep a close eye or strain the brain. We were blacktopping the last kilometre of the existing track, before tackling the rock face. The day seemed never ending. At last it was dusk. I had dinner with Rini. Shukra did make a passing remark about being abandoned, with a twinkle in his eyes. I could not think of any appropriate response. Rini blushed. We had the evening to ourselves, and after dinner strolled away from the camp for some privacy. By the time we returned the camp was asleep, and a few dying embers lay testimony to that evening's campfire.

The next morning Shukra asked most of the labour force to take the morning off. He took me to the rock face, and carried drills and explosives with him. He showed me how to charge the rock face with explosives, what effect to anticipate from the blast, and then fired the explosives from a safe distance. There was a thunderous noise followed by the rumbling of cascading rocks and pebbles, and a splash from down below when the debris hit the water of the stream. The slope of the mountainside disintegrated, leaving a wide irregular jagged ledge for some thirty yards. We came back to the camp, had lunch, and went back towing Ashwini in his bulldozer with us. Ashwini used the bulldozer to clear most of the loose rocks and boulders, feeding them to the stone crusher. After another couple of hours Shukra drilled into the rocks, and placed the explosives in strategic placements to achieve maximum effect. He fired the explosives, and broke off for the day. We headed back for the camp, and Shukra fell in beside me.

"Let the effect of the blast settle down. Sometimes the shock waves from the explosion loosen rocks and earth that take a few hours to dislodge from its position, and shower on the unwary, burying them." Shukra tried to explain to me why he was breaking off early.

That evening after dinner, in the glow of the camp fire, we asked Shukra to tell us of any unusual experience or incident he had encountered in his long career in the Border Roads. Initially he was reluctant, but with persuasion he agreed:

"The Border Roads Organisation, a quasi army and civilian organisation, was in its infancy and was tasked with building and maintenance of all mountainous roads in the sub-Himalayan region, the terrain mostly forms borders or line of control with neighbouring countries, namely China and Pakistan. I was posted in Project Vartak, in Arunachal Pradesh, in the North Eastern Frontier Area of India, notorious for insurgency and lack of communications. The year was 1969, monsoon had left the rest of the country, but low clouds maintained a weepy atmosphere with sodden earth and dripping foliage, making travel in this difficult terrain arduous and time consuming and tedious."

"Though I was posted at Tezpur, I was temporarily attached to the Task Force Headquarter at Tezu. I was unfortunate enough to be the only officer in the camp, and not out with a Road Construction Company or a survey team. I was ordered to distribute pay to the Task Force personnel and the labourers. Thus one morning when the sky was pouring buckets of water and visibility was restricted to a hundred yards at most, I led a contingent of pioneers, porters and an armed detachment of Assam Rifles into the wilderness, driving a convoy of five four-wheel drive jeeps, praying that the soggy earth had mercy on us and allowed sufficient grip to the wheels of our jeeps. Our workforce was scattered over a large hostile territory, with sparse communication, practically non-existent roads and insurgent Naga and mezo rebels in full cry."

"Meghalaya and Arunachal probably receive more rainfall than anywhere else in the world. The terrain is mountainous with lush vegetation and criss-crossed mountain streams. Most of the year, low hanging clouds and drizzle reduce visibility, and occasional cloud bursts cause flash floods. Being in the tropics, twilight is very short, with rapid transformation from daylight to pitch darkness."

"This Task Force was building and developing a highway from Hunli to Roing, a distance of approximately a hundred and fifty kilometres through and over mountains, thick forests and wild rivers: A daunting task for any brave-heart. Roing is the Capital city of Arunachal Pradesh, and Hunli, though a small village of uncertain population happens to be only three kilometres from the Chinese border, and of some considerable strategic importance to the military hierarchy. It is of course interesting to note that China does not recognise this border, and opposes the idea of the MacMohan line that the British in their zealous spirit had arbitrarily drawn on the globe through this inhospitable terrain, separating their Empire from China. Tension across the border was high, but more lethal were the ambushes staged by the insurgents, fighting for autonomy of the region since independence."

"Most of the staff and labour force were strung out along this road, in the process of being constructed and access to the camps varied from a jeep ride to a couple of days trudge across soggy squelchy and drenching landscape. We were carrying a large amount of money, and were a very attractive target to the rebels. We also had to be careful not to disturb poisonous snakes or wild animals. At the end of the days march, we were busy detaching leeches from ourselves, that had clung to us unnoticed and got fat sucking our blood. The Roing-Hunli Road followed the contours of the ridges, and lay at a variable height of nine to eleven thousand feet above sea level."

"We had spent the night before at 'Kilometer 32', a landmark in this expanse of uninhabited land, where a milestone reminds us that we are thirty two kilometres from Hunli. We had walked the whole day, and neared the labour camp well after Sun down. We pitched our tents by torch light, not daring to approach the labour camp by night, as there was a good chance that we may be shot at due to mistaken identity. It was safer in those days (and may be even now) to shoot first and ask questions later, for to try the other way was inviting death. Next morning after breakfast we approached the camp, and met the officer in charge, Assistant Engineer Peter Desouza. He was very hospitable, and warmly welcomed us (after all we brought his pay 'cash': though it was a different matter that he had no where to spend it other than gambling). We set up a distribution point at the labour camp, after descending a hundred feet from the road surface along a track clinging to the steep slope. It was easy to understand why Mr Desouza chose that particular spot as the labour camp. It was the only meadow in the area with a gentle slope, and large enough to accommodate so many people. A mountain stream hugged one edge of the perimeter of the meadow, providing easy access to drinking water. The meadow was surrounded by tall trees and thick undergrowth of shrubs, making silent approach to the camp difficult for insurgents or wild animals. Mr Desouza split the workforce into two groups, one group was to work in the morning and clear the debris from the previous night's blast, while the second group would work in the afternoon, after collecting their pay. There were over a thousand people to pay, but through excellent management, we completed distribution well before dark."

"This camp was tasked to do formation cutting: that is creating a path through the mountain, wide enough to be converted into a highway. They would clear the previous night's debris, and then dig holes to put charge against the mountain slope. They would return to camp before dark, and after a head count to ensure that everyone was safe, the charges would be fired in succession, blowing away rocks and earth and vegetation to leave a flat surface where the slope existed. Rock fall would continue through most of the night. The sub-Himalayan region is prone to earthquakes, and this blasting probably helped to destabilise the area, inviting more tremors."

"We had dinner with the men at the camp, and walked up to Mr Desouza's quarters, a good hundred metres climb from the labour camp, through dimly lit game trail. A couple of porters carried the money chest behind us, to place it under the bed. A folding cot was sprung for me, and I spread my sleeping bag on it. It was quite dark by the time Subedar-Major reported that all was well, and that all camp lights were snuffed out (except ours of course). The time was half past eight. We sat on a couple of rickety chairs in the glow of a kerosene lamp heightening the gloom. We were busy updating each other of events and gossips, when there was a knock on the door. The double door was not very strong, consisting mostly of wooden panels, with a glass window pane for the top panel. I turned around to face the door, as the knock was repeated. Mr Desouza called out to identify the person at the door, but there was no reply. Intrigued and fearful of insurgents, at Desouza's request, I opened the door. I could not see any one. The cabin, made up of corrugated metal sheets and wood was fifteen feet long and ten feet wide, including a toilet at the back of the room we were in. It was constructed on a ledge, leaving barely five feet in all directions. The back was a sheer cliff, covered with vegetation. The sides sloped steeply with grassy banks and the front approach was a narrow track climbing from the road at a fairly steep gradient. Approach was practically impossible from any direction but the front. We took a torch each, and searched the ledge for anyone hiding. Finding no one, we went back into the hut, and resumed our discussion. Ten minutes late, the knock sounded again. This time I saw the hand knocking the glass panel. Again we repeated the search without any success. I was puzzled. I locked the door. Another ten minutes and again the hand knocked our door. I looked at Desouza. He gently shook his head and asked me to ignore it. I was intrigued, and asked him what was going on. He said that over the past few years, strange incidents have happened on nights before any major accident happened in the camp. He said that he had no doubt in his mind that we were going to have an accident the next day. I did not believe him. I was convinced that he had arranged this to scare me and have fun at my expense. After all stuck in this remote corner, he may have developed a weird sense of humour."

"I had to change my mind the next morning when Subedar-Major told us that the first group of labourers to clear the debris sustained severe injuries from delayed blasting of some charges. Two men died on the spot, and the third had his right hand blown off. We rushed immediately to the road, where the casualties were being brought in. Desouza telephoned Tezu to get helicopters to evacuate the man to Tezpur Military Hospital. After the man was airlifted, and the camp quieted down, I bid goodbye to Desouza's and carrying the money chest with us walked back to our jeeps, on our way to the next camp."

Shukra finished his narrative, but we sat in silence reflecting on the eerie conclusion. The story touched a cord with most of the listeners, especially when we have to do our own new formation cutting over the next few days. Shukra gauged our mood, and broke up the camp saying that it was late, and we have work to do early next morning. I think Rini was feeling scared and clung to me until I deposited her unto her own tent mates.

In the morning every thing was back to normal, and the labourers moved all loose stones and boulders to the stone crusher. The bulldozer broke the uneven rocky projections, which were smoothed over with pickaxes and spades. For the next couple of kilometres the mountainside had a gentle slope, and blasting was not necessary. The rhythm of road making swung into full force, and within a couple of days the surface was a smooth shiny black curvaceous serpent, hugging the slopes. Shukra had gone forward, and was blasting rocky outcrops that he thought was more than the bulldozer could cope. He stayed well ahead to spare us from being hit by flying rocks or rolling boulders. I was following him with the labour force, building a wide blacktop road as we progressed.

The last kilometre of the projected road had to be carved out of almost vertical, precipitous cliffs. Shukra wanted to carve a hollow from the side, and support the overhang with concrete pillars. He asked me if I had head for heights. I answered in the affirmative. We climbed to the top of the cliff, and Shukra, with the help of a few strong men and pulleys lowered me with nylon ropes to a height similar to the road surface along the cliff face. I drilled a series of holes, at intervals of five metres, and charged them with explosives. I was hauled up, and we returned to a safe place before firing the explosives. As expected, a chunk of rock from the middle of the cliff was sliced off, leaving an overhang. We returned to the camp. Shukra's plan was to get the masons to erect concrete pillars at intervals of five metres to support the cliff where it formed the overhang.

That evening, as has been the routine of late, I had my dinner with Rini, and we went for a stroll. We were talking sweet nothing, and were oblivious to the world around us. Unknowingly, or perhaps subconsciously we walked towards the overhang. In the dark nothing much was visible. Locating a convenient spot off the road, we sat down under a tree. I put my head on Rini's lap and the world appeared at peace. I do not know how long we were there, when a slight tremor of the earth and distant rumble startled us. I stood up, and went towards the stream to investigate. Suddenly the sound intensified, and I realised what it was. It was a landslide.

"Run Rini", I heard myself shouting. My voice drowned in the crescendo of falling boulders. I was hit and felt myself falling over the edge of the cliff. I fell for a second or two, time moved in slow motion. My back hit something, and I was tearing through foliage. Suddenly something hit the back of my head, and blackness surrounded me. I lost consciousness.

SHUKRA ORAON

The evening was quiet. It was getting late. We had our dinner a couple of hours ago. I had doused our camp fires and had retired to my tent. Rajiv had not returned yet, probably out with Rini. It felt good to have young people around me, made me feel less old. I was reflecting over the days work. We had done a lot of blasting today. The slope was very steep, and we had carved out a hollow. I had an uneasy feeling. I wanted to support the overhang with concrete pillars as soon as possible to stabilise the mountainside. I must have dozed off. A sudden tremor shook the Earth, and woke me up. Probably an earthquake, I thought: left my bed and came out of the tent. Small tremors are quite frequent in these mountains. A deep rumble echoed around the hills, and sent a shiver of chill down my spine. I knew what it was; I had heard it many times before. A landslide is sweeping down the slopes, eliminating everything in its path. The ground under my feet resonated with the rumble and the crash. All the labourers were awake now, standing outside their tents: some in fear, some in awe, and some in the knowledge of the catastrophe. I quickly realised that we were safe, and that the landslide was happening some distance away from our camp site. The site of the new blasting that we did today sprung to my mind as the most likely area.

For almost half an hour we stood in the dark, exaggerated by the flickering light of a couple of lanterns, staring at each other and listening to the deep rumble and splashing of rocks falling into the gorge as the Earth tore itself. I knew there was nothing I could do until the Earth had settled. I did not see Rajiv or Rini in the crowd, and decided to do a roll call to check who were missing. It was nearly midnight, and everyone except the young couple was in camp. I had a strong premonition of disaster. I tried to stay calm, and asked for a few volunteers to light up all the lanterns and pick up all the electric torches. We also took a folding stretcher with us, and a first aid kit.

We were very familiar with the area, and darkness did not impede us. We walked briskly towards the new formation cutting. There was an eerie silence around us, once the stragglers amongst the falling rocks had settled down. The preceding earth-shattering crash made the silence even more poignant. We walked in silence, each of us mulling over our own thoughts. We were on schedule with the work, and another two weeks would have seen us packing our camp and heading for the base. Now, depending on the scale of the damage we may have to stay on for a few more weeks, until snow made work near impossible. Only by daylight one can tell the extent of the devastation.

As we neared the site, we could see rock piles on the new road even in the darkness, as ghostly mounds, breaking the silhouette of the slope and the ledge we had laboured to create. Closer to the rock-fall, we shouted names. The dancing torch lights showed that the overhang had completely collapsed, leaving a wide ledge, piled high with boulders and debris. I asked everyone to stop shouting, to spread out, and listen. I also warned everyone not to take any unnecessary risk, or approach the cliff edge.

Someone shouted and flashed his torch in my direction. I hurried over to where he was pointing. He was looking at a jumble of rocks.

As I approached, I heard a groan. I called everyone, and asked them to remove the stones by hand. I did not hear any more sound. At times I wondered if I had imagined the noise. We persisted, and continued to rollaway the boulders and debris. Eventually I saw a human figure. From the clothes I could identify Rini. She had fainted, at least I hoped so. After she was uncovered, I noticed that her right leg was at an odd angle, and there was a lot of blood at the spot. She had bruises and lacerations else where, but her face was remarkably preserved. We gently put her on the stretcher, straightened her leg and tucked her in with blankets. I left a few men to look for Rajiv, and carried Rini back to the camp.

In the camp I used a pair of scissors to cut Rini's 'salwar' and expose the leg. I wished I had not. The leg was crushed and mangled below the knee, flesh and bone pieces were hanging with shreds of skin. I soaked some clean cloth with rum, and covered the wound, a crude attempt at minimising infection, more in hope than based on any medical evidence. She looked pale and was not responding. I realised that she did not have much time, and needed urgent medical attention. I picked up the field telephone and rang the BRTF Headquarter. I spoke to the Commander, Brigadier Mathews. He was a career officer in the Engineering corps, on deputation to Border Roads for three years. Briefly I explained the situation, and asked him to request an Air Force helicopter to evacuate Rini to the Army hospital at Simla. Though the labourers are on daily wages, and not part of either the Border Roads or the Army, in disaster situations like this accident victims are often treated in Army Hospitals. I still had not heard anything about Rajiv, and my hopes were sinking.

Despite the lateness of the hour, nearly an hour later we heard a helicopter. I went out, and asked the men and women to form a large circle, pointing their torches towards the helicopter. As the helicopter landed, even before the rotors had stopped, an army doctor jumped out, followed by a nursing assistant. With a stooping run, they came towards the camp. I met them and took them to my tent where Rini lay on the stretcher. She had come round, and was whimpering in pain. The doctor did a quick examination, lifted the cloth from her shattered leg and replaced it after a look. He shot Rini with a large dose of morphine in her left thigh, and asked us to take the stretcher to the helicopter. We swapped stretchers, taking one from the helicopter, keeping Rini on the original stretcher, and loading her onto the helicopter. Within minutes they were off, leaving a dusty smell of aviation fuel and a distant fading clatter of the rotors.

I deployed a small search party to look for Rajiv near the spot where Rini was found, and sent everyone else to bed. The next few days were going to be very hectic, and I wanted them to get as much rest as possible. I snatched a few hours sleep, and early next morning, taking a fresh party of men with me, went down to the river bank. There was mostly a very narrow ledge on the side of the river, and in places the sides consisted of sheer cliffs. We waded water and had to struggle to keep our balance against the freezing current of the fast flowing water. The rock fall had caused a small dam, backing up water and slowing the flow. At the site of the rock-fall, the sides of the river consisted of sheer cliffs a hundred feet high. We searched until we were exhausted and chilled to our bones, but did not see any trace of Rajiv. Looking up to the cliff top, it was quite apparent that any one falling through that height had very little chance of survival, and even if he did, the ice cold water would cause hypothermia. The fast current would propel the hapless victim against sharp rocky outcrops on its headlong dash towards the plains, and would batter the body beyond any possibility of survival. In a perverse way that gave me a glimmer of hope. Perhaps Rajiv was trapped in the rock fall like Rini, on the ledge under the overhang. It was a slim chance, and I recognised it as such, but as long as hope is not completely snuffed out, even a flicker can give the illusion of a warm glow. A human mind is forever the optimist, and latches onto even the faintest of possibilities, building assurances, refusing at times to accept logical explanations and evidence. If one gives up hope, nothing remains. I had become much attached to Rajiv, and just could not accept the fact that he may be no more. How was I going to face Rini!

The crystal clear water bared its bed to anyone willing to see. The white sandy bottom with rows of black stones did not hide anything. Even the shoals of trout meandering in the water could not find shadowy crevices to hide from prying eyes. At last I had to give up. We found a flat rock, and build a fire to warm our numb bodies. We could barely talk through the chattering teeth. By dusk we returned to our camp. The group searching amongst the rocky mounds on the ledge were equally unsuccessful and frustrated. I handed out some encouraging words and platitudes, and a large helping of rum. We had a subdued dinner, and wrapped our blankets, drifting off to dreamless, death like sleep, the sleep of exhaustion.

I had to make a decision. I accepted that Rajiv must be dead. He probably fell off the cliff, and the fast flowing river swept him downstream. Firstly there was very little chance of his surviving the fall, and secondly even if he did, the freezing water of the river would cause hypothermia; not to mention the possibility of being torn and battered against rocky outcrops as the fast current swept him downstream.

I had sent men up to ten miles down the river to find out if his body was snagged in the river, or was seen by anyone. Again there was no news.

I had to concentrate on the work at hand. Thoughts of Rajiv were always with me, and I felt a terrible loss. As the days went by, I had managed to get a better grip on myself, and had to accept that Rajiv was no more. I knew very little about his background, and had no idea who his next of kin was. Rajiv had been very close mouthed about his family, and evaded direct questions.

The accident had done me a great favour. It had created a ledge much wider than any amount of blasting could have done, and I finished the road works a week before time. I handed over the responsibility of winding down the operation to one my subordinate assistant engineers, whom I had originally tasked to monitor the maintenance of Joshimath-Badrinath road. I requested for an attachment to the 'Project Deepak' Headquarter at Simla, and was granted permission. I wanted to settle down in Simla after retirement, and it made sense to spend as much time there before retirement as possible, to arrange for accommodation, and to generally get to know the place, familiarise with local residents. I also wanted to be close to Rini, who was still being treated at the Military Hospital there.

I went to Simla as an administrative officer to the Project headquarters, in the planning directorate. I was more anxious to meet Rini than knowing what my new job entailed. I put in my application for early retirement, planning to leave by the end of the year.

I went to see Rini that evening. Rini was in the female surgical ward. She looked pale and thin and withdrawn. She was reclining in her bed, eyes closed. She looked tired, with dark rings under her eyes. She looked serene and beautiful in repose. I pulled up a chair next to her bed, and taking her hand in mine I called her name softly: "Rini."

She opened her eyes. A questioning look with slightly raised eyebrows greeted me. I understood her, and gently shook my head.

"We did not find him," Was my inadequate reply.

She closed her eyes again, and tears started streaming down her cheek. She made no sound.

"Rini," I gently called her.

"I lost my right leg," She said opening her eyes. "Why should I live?" What should I live for?"

The meeting was proving to be even more emotionally draining than I had anticipated. I knew the doctors had to take her to the operation theatre that night. She had lost a lot of blood. She had to have a below knee amputation of her right leg. She needed blood transfusions.

"Only her youth and resilience and courage had saved her." One of the doctors had told me. "She is very depressed and needs emotional support. She is not eating, only picking at her food. The wound is healing nicely, but very soon she will have to co-operate with the physiotherapists to learn to use the crutches, and to rehabilitate. She must first of all accept the reality."

"I understand your pain," I said to Rini, "But you must try to be strong. If Rajiv was here today, that is what he would have expected of you, and not a whimpering weakling, I am sure!"

I knew I was being harsh, but I had to get her out of the state of self pity that she was indulging in at the time.

"You have to be strong for his sake, and for mine. I need your company and your beautiful voice. I want you to come and stay with me now that I am retiring. That is what Rajiv wanted anyway."

I spent a few more hours with her, talking to her, asking her about the past, her aspirations and ambitions before the accident, and in general trying to focus her mind away from the misery, towards a goal.

I left her that evening, depressed. I realised I had an up hill struggle on my hands if I wanted Rini to be the self confident, laughing, giving and caring person she was. I had to think of a prop that would take her mind away from Rajiv and the accident. I went to the hospital every evening after work, and spent hours with Rini. I coaxed and cajoled her to cooperate with the physiotherapists. I managed to make her take a few tentative steps. I took membership of the local district library and borrowed fictions and works of well known authors and autobiographies and read them to her. I tried to entertain her by reminiscing and recounting anecdotes from my past, difficulties and hardships and tragedies faced by others. I wanted her to understand that adversity is a part of life, and we should take it in our stride, looking for and creating a better and brighter and wiser future for ourselves, and all around us. One small success is neither the end of the road, nor the aim of our life, but the endeavour to always achieve something better should be our guiding philosophy in life.

On Sundays and at other times whenever I got the opportunity, I was house hunting. I had spread the word, and was getting feed backs. I had seen a few properties but none of them had appealed to me. I was looking for a cottage or a bungalow with a good view across the valley and of the majestic Himalayan peaks. One day I was walking along a track, and suddenly as I topped a hill, the panoramic view in front held me spellbound. The afternoon Sun reflected off the lofty snowy peaks towering over green hill tops. Grazing cattle dotting the valley basked in the warmth. Next morning I went to the land registry office to locate the owner of the valley.

A month slipped by. Time flew. Rini was still reluctant to cooperate fully with the physiotherapists. My scolding and pleading did get her out of bed and on to the crutches, but her heart was not in her efforts. Progress was understandably very slow. Rini rarely spoke, responding in monosyllables when spoken to. She had withdrawn into a shell, and lived mostly in her own world. She showed no interest in her surroundings. The wound had healed well. My retirement papers had gone through, and I got permission to take terminal leave from end of December. I bought the plot of land, and had engaged a local builder to construct a small chalet in keeping with the local architecture. He promised me the construction work will be complete within a couple of months. I did not have any problem with the planning permission. It appeared that the local corporation had set aside that sector of land for future residential development. It was on the outskirts of the town, and only a dirt track reached my new home to be. I was assured that electricity and water supply would be established as soon as the construction was complete. In fact they had started laying the pipes and cables. Everything was progressing smoothly, only Rini worried me.

On a cold November Sunday morning I was strolling on the 'Mall' along the parapet wall, enjoying the golden reflection of the rising Sun off the snowy peaks, when an elderly gentleman touched my elbow, and broke my revere.

"Excuse me please, are you Mister Oraon?" He asked, and added "I am Shridhar Pandit."

"Yes, what can I do for you?" I replied, appraising the intruder. He was in his early sixties with white back-brushed hair. He was wearing an 'Aligarhi' with his 'Kurta' and wrapped a Kashmiri shawl around him. His right hand was by his side, but the left elbow was flexed to support the shawl. He wore steel rimmed glasses. He was as tall as me though a bit heavier and wider around his middle: or may be the shawl was creating an illusion of girth.

"I am going to be your neighbour," he said. "I purchased a plot of land near yours, where you are constructing your house."

"Namaste," I greeted him in the traditional way.

"I was born and brought up in Simla," he continued. "My father was a central government employee, and was posted out to Delhi when I was in my senior school. Until recently, I was a professor at Jawaharlal Nehru University in Classical Indian Music. I have now retired, and wish to settle here. I am with my wife. Our children have scattered, as seems to be the norm these days," he paused. "Are you here with your family?" He asked. "My wife would love to have some company."

"I must disappoint your wife, I am afraid," I said. "I lost my wife long ago, and my son is in the army. However, I shall be living with my foster daughter, who recently had a tragic accident. In fact, I may solicit your professional help in future to rehabilitate her."

We made polite conversation, talked of local and national politics, inflation and life in general. We parted, going in our separate ways, promising to meet soon. He gave me his present address; he had rented the property for six months.

Over the next few weeks I visited him a few times, met his wife, and spent some time discussing Rini. I asked Shridhar if he would consider taking up the challenge and try to interest Rini to pursue a career in music. He agreed to give it a try.

After two months in hospital, Rini was ready for discharge. She had learned to walk with the crutches, though she remained depressed and spoke only in monosyllables. She was still wrapped up in her own world, reluctant to come out of her shell. I warned Shridhar that he was in for a tough time.

One evening I invited the Pandits and introduced them to Rini. During the evening Rini was attentive but quiet, not joining in any conversation. Sudha, Shridhar's wife, tried to draw her out, but was not very successful.

At last the day came when my house was eventually ready to move in. I threw a house warming party, calling the Pandits and a few of my colleagues from the Project Headquarters. As usual Rini was quiet and withdrawn. After dinner, we sat around and someone started to sing. After two or three performances Sudha requested Rini to sing. She was reluctant initially, but when I supported the request, she could not refuse. She sang a simple popular song, mechanically, devoid of any emotions. Later Shridhar acknowledged that Rini had a nice voice, but needed a lot of coaching. Sudha was quite drawn to Rini, and tried all evening to get her to open up, without much success.

Days were shorter and colder with mist and frequent rain and snow falls. The track in front of our house had become slushy and slippery. I had to stop our afternoon ritual of a small walk to the top of the hill, where Rini and I would sit quietly for some time and then we would trace our way back home. I did the weekly shopping, and Rini cooked for both of us. Shridhar and Sudha were still staying in their rented accommodation, their house was incomplete. Their builder had stopped work, and was going to start again in spring when the weather improved. The weather was wet windy and unpredictable. We wore woollens most of the time, and burnt an electric heater to keep us warm.

Once a week I made a trip to the local library, and picked up fictions, poetry and occasionally biographies of great men. I often tried to inspire Rini, citing examples of overcoming hardship. My constant company was having some effect. Probably she started to take pity on this old man. Whatever the reason, Rini started to speak more often and even smiled at times. Our television reception was not good, but videos of Hindi and English films helped to while away the long dark winter evenings. Most evenings I insisted that Rini sang a few songs to me. I bought audio cassettes of old and newly released popular film songs. It was a slow progress, but the black veil of melancholy was gradually drifting away. Rini was becoming quite adept at using her crutches, and could move easily. We had fallen into a set routine, and in the late afternoon, if the weather was good, we would go for a short walk up the path, and sit on a flat rock at the top of the hill and gaze at the enchanting vista around us.

"Rini," I asked gently one afternoon, "Would you like to take up music? I think you will find peace and satisfaction if you could focus your mind away from the accident."

"I have been thinking about it." Rini said.

"Give it a try," I encouraged her. "You know, Shridhar has agreed to coach you in Indian Classical Music. It takes a lot of time, effort and dedication to master that art."

"Alright," She agreed. "What do I have to do now?"

"Don't worry about it. I'll speak to Shridhar and make the arrangements. I would also like you to go back to formal education. You don't have to go to school, you can take the exams privately, and if needed I can arrange a tutor for you."

"Won't that be expensive?" She asked.

"I can afford it." I said. "I had promised Rajiv that I'll look after you, and that is my only responsibility in life at present."

"What about your son and grandchildren?"

"My son is old enough and capable enough to look after himself and his family."

Rini remained silent, staring at the distant setting Sun, gradually disappearing behind the western silhouetted peaks. It was getting chilly. As long as the Sun remained bright, it was pleasant outside. With the Sun loosing its vigour, a restless breeze set off eddies among dried leaves. I wrapped my shawl tighter around my shoulders, and stood up. I extended my right hand towards Rini and said,

"Let's go. It will be dark soon."

"I like to see the Sunset from here" Rini said. "But you are right it is getting a bit nippy. I don't want you to catch a cold," She quipped.

Gripping my hand, she pulled herself up on her leg. I handed her the crutches, and slowly walked back to our chalet.

I switched on the television to watch the evening news. Rini went into the kitchen, and started preparing our dinner. Over the past month I had been trying to keep her as busy as possible, and now let her do all the housework herself.

Suddenly Rini popped into the lounge and asked "Can I call you Dadaji?"

"You can call me whatever you like, as long as you show some respect for my age." I laughed.

She seemed happy with my answer, and went back to the kitchen. Presently she emerged again, pushing the food trolley, and declared: "Dinner is served!"

I went to the toilet, washed my hands and face, and joined her on the table. After a long time I saw glimpses of the old Rini in her. I hoped that the melancholia was receding for good. It was simple but a tasty fare, lovingly prepared, and consumed with relish. I praised her cooking. She ignored me, and started asking about Shridhar. I told her whatever I knew. I was pleased to see her interest.

A month after her discharge from the hospital, I took her back for review. The surgeon, lieutenant colonel Ansari, was quite pleased with her progress. He asked me if I could take her to Pune Artificial Limb Centre. I was delighted at the prospect, and readily agreed.

"There is a fair bit of wait for the limbs to arrive," Lt. Col Ansari said. "You will have to go initially for the measurement, and about six months later they will call you for limb fitting. She will have to stay there for a month to undergo intensive physiotherapy and acclimatisation, to get used to the new attachment. The Artificial Limb Centre has accommodation for relatives at a nominal daily rate. You will have very little expense. Even your railway fare from Simla to Pune will be reimbursed.

Our happiness knew no bounds. Rini hugged me with joy, and started crying. On Lt.Col Ansari's advice, I wrote a letter to the Artificial Limb Centre, and attached a copy of the referral letter, to inform them that we were coming for the measurements. I booked the earliest reservation available in 'Jhelum-Express' from New Delhi to Pune. I had to buy a separate ticket for Simla to Delhi. Simla to Pune involved one change of trains at New Delhi, nearly forty hours of travel time through two thousand kilometres of varied terrain, starting in the Himalayan foothills, and crossing through the middle of the Indian peninsula to reach the 'Western Ghats'. I had booked two berths in a second class three tier sleeper compartment. We took an overnight train to New Delhi. After refreshing ourselves in the railway retiring room and indulging in a sumptuous breakfast of 'puri-sabji', we caught the Jhelum Express at eleven in the morning.

Our compartment was clean and well lighted. There were ten cubicles on one side of the passage, with six berths to each cubicle.

The other side of the passage had a bunk bed type of arrangement, placed lengthwise next to the windows, corresponding to the width of the cubicle. The berths in the cubicles were placed at right angles to the length of the compartment, and one end was adjacent to the windows, while the gap between the other ends formed the entrance to the cubicle from the passage. Three bunks (Upper, middle and lower) were lined on either side of the cubicle, the passage and the windows forming the other limits. The cubicles were separated by thin wooden partitions. The lower bunk or berth is where the passengers sit during the day, and the top bunk holds the luggage. The middle berth is folded away during the day to facilitate passengers to sit comfortably. At night however, the middle berth is swung up to a horizontal position on its hinges, and slung with steel chains from the struts holding the top bunk. Once the middle berth is deployed, sitting on the lower berth becomes very uncomfortable due to lack of headroom. Luggage from the top berth is pulled down and put under the lower berth, or on the floor space in the middle of the cubicle. All six berths are used for lying down to sleep by the passengers, one to each berth.

Across the aisle, the lower berth is pulled back to form two chairs for passengers to sit on, but at night, sliding panels are pulled across the seat to cover the gap. One of the passengers occupying a chair has to climb up to the top bunk.

There were two toilets, one on each side of the compartment, and two hand basins, each snugly fitted in an alcove adjacent to the door on the side of the cubicles. All compartments were interconnected, and passengers, hawkers and ticket checkers could walk the length of the train quite easily. At night the interconnecting doors were locked for security reasons. This arrangement was quite popular with long distance passengers who preferred to sleep comfortably at night, yet sit and chat during the day. If anyone wished to lie down during the day, he or she had to climb up to the top bunk. Since these compartments were reserved, no more than six people were allocated to each cubicle and two across the aisle. There were no overcrowding, and despite the length and duration of the journey, travel was reasonably comfortable and cheap.

Our train left on time, and we rapidly passed through the industrial belt around Delhi. The train slowed down after we crossed the oil refinery at Mathura for a brief stop. The day was warming up as the Sun climbed to its zenith. The windows were fully open, and as the train picked up speed, it generated a pleasant breeze. Bright Sunshine with a hint of dust haze lay outside. Small villages and clumps of vegetation slipped past. Grinning children waved at us. Farmers were too busy tilling the land, preparing it for the next crop. Dry riverbeds and streams criss-crossed the landscape. Suddenly I glimpsed the shinny white monument standing in all its magnificence across the wide expanse of the Yamuna. The River was low in water, and the sandy banks formed most of the expanse. Its minarets and its symmetry, its form and its architecture, seen so many times on postcards and posters, televisions and films: there was no need to tell any one. The Taj Mahal, monument to love and beauty, standing by the banks of the River Yamuna for the past four centuries does not need any introduction to Indians. It grew smaller and smaller, and then the view was obscured. No matter how many times I saw it, every time the sight presented a freshness of beauty, an elation of spirit and filled me with a sense of awe.

As the Sun slanted westward we entered the Chambal valley: strewn with ravines, famous for harbouring and hiding dacoits. Until recently the neighbouring villages were terrorised by these mounted lawless murdering gangs. The law enforcing authorities were helpless. The terrain aided undetectable movements through the ravines, and hideouts in the mountains. The soft sand of the dried riverbeds dampened all sound of movement and the high shoulders of the narrow ravines kept mounted riders out of sight. The interconnected ravines provided a safe corridor for unnoticed silent movement. These ravines cover hundreds of square kilometres. It is quite easy to get lost here without local knowledgeable help. The dacoits were armed, and did not hesitate to engage the police in armed combat. The social inequality and poverty of the region fed a steady stream of new recruits to strengthen these gangs. They have their own territories mapped out, and protect their turf with unusual ferocity.

The Vindhyachal Mountain ranges that separate the Indo-Gangetic plain of northern India from the Deccan Plateau in the south are much older than the Himalayas and erosion and weathering is much in evidence. The mountain tops are mostly flat mesas, with sometimes precipitous drop to the floor of the ravines.

The Sun gradually lost its glare as it sank towards the western horizon, eventually leaving pink and crimson and purple hues in the sky, colouring a few scattered lonely floating clouds. Darkness followed swiftly. The breeze lost its warmth, and a hint of chill crept in.

Our train stopped at Jhansi. Food trays were loaded into the pantry car. Some passengers got down on the platform to stretch their legs, others to crowd the vendors cooking hot food on their mobile kitchen units. These are the ones who either do not trust the railways to feed them on time, or do not like the fixed menu, preferring to eat off the vendors on the platform. They certainly have a wide choice. Still others were looking at trinkets to carry as souvenirs for their loved ones. The train had a ten minutes scheduled stop here to allow change of guard and drivers, load up food and also to top up water. The pantry car was not equipped to cook for hundreds of hungry passengers. The waiters took advanced orders, and relayed the message ahead. Catering contractors deliver the required quantity of fixed menu food at designated stations. The system works very well. The food is usually served at the seat, when the train has left the station and is on the move. The food is hot, filling, tasty and cheap. Sweet dish in the form of yoghurt or ice-cream is also served separately. Many passengers left the train, their places taken by new arrivals.

Travellers on Indian trains are a friendly talkative lot, especially the women, who are very inquisitive about their fellow passengers. Being a captive audience, it is very difficult to avoid personal questions without being very rude. Personal intrusion is not their intention, they just want to while away the long hours, and talk on familiar subjects. By the time a few hours have elapsed, passengers in a cubicle will usually get to know each other fairly well. Former strangers would join in card games, or be involved in animated, often heated political discussions. Listening to fragments of conversations one can be excused for assuming that the compartment has specialists in every field under the Sun. Everyone has ready advice and remedies for all ailments. Advice is readily, even eagerly given with promise of guaranteed results. Anecdotes would be thrown in to authenticate and substantiate tall claims. Trying to find common friends and matchmaking is perhaps the most popular pastime among the women.

Our train was travelling South through central India, towards the Western Ghats, which formed one of the sides of the triangular Deccan Plateau. Flat cultivated and semi arid land gave way to mountainous broken landscape, with undulation and forestry. As we approached the 'Ghats', the hills became more prominent, and the train had to pass through a few tunnels. Waterfalls and river bridges were occasionally encountered. Pylons carrying high voltage electricity and a snaking black road were running parallel to the railway line, and kept us constant company. Being a dry season, the land was parched and brown, except where modern farm irrigation methods were being used, pumping water through deep tube-wells.

Next to me sat a young man in his early twenties, travelling to Pune for a job interview. He was a chemist, and had done his graduation with honours from Aligarh Muslim University. He was hoping to land a job in a pharmaceutical manufacturing company at Pimpri. The position he was going for was a lucrative post, with a good salary and perks. He expected stiff competition in the interview. He was subdued and tense, speaking in monosyllables only when spoken to. In my effort to divert his mind and engage him in a conversation, I asked him some probing questions. My age gave me the license to carry it off.

It transpired that he was the eldest of a large family; all his siblings were either in school or university. His father had just retired from a modest job. Though they owned their ancestral home in Aligarh, the cost of living was quite high and his father's pension was not stretching far enough. The family had high expectations of him. He had two sisters, and though it was likely that they would become earning members soon, he was expected to contribute heavily towards their marriage. The dowry system, though illegal, persist in their community and the girl's family has to contribute heavily towards the settlement, often forcing the bride's parents or brothers to sell their home. Over the years this evil practice has eased in many communities, but is still fairly prevalent in most parts of India.

The dowry system probably started quite innocuously, as the bride's father extending a helping hand to the newly weds to settle down. Over the years the practice, especially in some communities, has been taken for granted. So much so, that the groom's family submit a list of demands, with the threat that failure to meet the demand will result in cancellation of the marriage. The failure to meet the demand is also seen as loss of standing of the bride's family in that community, and probably ranks high as one of the causes of high incidence of bribery in India.

This practice has grown like a cancerous growth in the Indian communities, and has ruined many a family. As a fall out, other vicious practices like blackmailing the bride's family even after marriage and bride burning are often in the news. Where a bride's family failed or refused to pay up the demands made after marriage, there has been incidences the bride has been murdered under the guise of home accident, and the groom remarried to gain more wealth. Initially even the police was quite helpless to act due to lack of evidence, until the government acted decisively to enact laws that put the onus on the groom's family to prove that the accident was not homicide. The police was empowered to arrest the groom and his immediate family on suspicion. Some couples resort to female infanticide or abortion of female foetuses to avoid these situations.

The changes in the law did have some restraining effect on these practices, but the practice still lives on underground. In a country where unemployment is high, someone having a steady or high income is in high demand. Most people realise that the only way to kill this malignant system is to empower women to be high earners, and gain economic freedom. The necessary change in culture has started, but may take generations to come through, especially in the lower middle class families, where women are still not equipped mentally and academically to be financially independent.

I felt pity for the young man. Even before he had a chance to taste freedom, heavy burden of responsibility and social slavery was thrust on his young shoulders. Some can carry it off with élan and create a niche for themselves in this world, while others are driven to desperation, finding solace in drugs, alcohol and suicide.

The sixth passenger in our cubicle was a soldier returning home on annual leave. He was posted in a non-family station, along the western border. The only identification of the location he was allowed to convey to his family was a postal address: 56 APO, which could be any where in the western half of the country, along with the names of his battalion and regiment. He is bound by the 'official secret act', and is reluctant to talk to strangers in case he inadvertently divulges information that the army might consider secret. It does not matter if the information is already in the public domain through the media or other sources, and is yesterday's news.

His family lives in Sholapur, and he will have to change trains at Pune for onward remaining journey. He had not seen his wife or other members of his family for nearly two years. All leave was cancelled the year before due to escalation of tension along the Indo-Pak line of control. When he last left home, his son was five years old, and his little daughter was learning to walk, making up funny words for things that caught her eye and the actual name defeated her tongue. She could identify him as her father, but he has doubts about her ability to do so now.

His father was in his seventies, and had diabetes. Earlier in the year he had received a letter from his wife saying that his father was not keeping well, complaining of chest pains and breathlessness. She had taken him to the nearest military hospital, where he was admitted for a couple of weeks. His mother needed an operation for cataract. He is entitled to two months annual leave every year, but does not always get it, especially when hostilities flare up between the neighbouring countries. Since it takes him three days of travel each way to and from his home, his commanding officer wanted him to take all annual leave in one bloc. He jumped at the offer, not knowing what the future holds. Most of his leave will be spent sorting out family problems, tending to the small farm and maintenance of the house. His younger brother looks after the farm, but income from it is never enough, and he has to contribute. He has been in the infantry battalion for the past seven years, and has had to move around a fair bit, depending on the exigencies of service.

A middle aged couple sat across the aisle. They carried a large picnic hamper, and a terracotta pot of cold drinking water. They were over weight, and it was easy to see why. Most of the journey they were dipping into the hamper for nibbles, in addition to ordering all the meals served by the railway, and buying tit bits from the vendors at stations. They were too engrossed with themselves, and except for occasional passing comments, were busy eating and snoring. They owned a grocery shop at Agra, and were on their way to Nasik to be with their daughter who is expecting soon. The shop is being looked after by their son for the time being. Their son in law had a retail textile business, and apparently was doing well.

Light was fast fading outside our windows. The train stopped from time to time for short intervals, maintaining a steady speed towards the south-west. I looked at my watch when the train reached Bina to pick up reserved hot food trays from the caterers, and noted that the train was running on schedule. Once the train picked up speed, the waiters served us according to our orders. The process was unbelievably smooth and efficient with no mix-up of orders. The empty plates were collected half an hour later, and were taken to the pantry car. We deployed the middle berth, and by ten that evening were lying flat on our backs, contemplating sleep.

Two cubicles further down the compartment, a large party of twenty adults and twelve children of various ages were travelling to attend a marriage. They appeared to be enjoying themselves. We could hear their boisterous laughter, heated debates and snatches of conversations. The conductor on duty walked down checking our tickets, and warned them to keep the noise level down. He did that more from optimism than hope, and I resigned myself to a disturbed sleep. However, by eleven they had quietened down, and I learnt the reason later. They had to get off at Igatpuri, at five in the morning.

As long as it was possible to see through the window, Rini was glued to it. As the darkness deepened and the air became cooler, she pulled down the glass shutter, and looked at me. I smiled at her and she gave me a sheepish grin. After dinner, she had helped me to make the beds. The train stopped at Bhusaval for ten minutes, to allow change of guards and drivers and also to refill the water tanks. Many passengers left the train and their places were taken by new arrivals.

I was sleeping on the lower berth. Though the windows were closed, a sudden chill woke me up. The train had pulled up at Igatpuri, and I could hear the party getting off the train. Igatpuri is probably the highest railway station on this line. I opened one of the windows, and bought a cup of hot tea from a passing vendor. I shut the window and looked at my watch. It was a few minutes past five in the morning. The sky was still dark, and the birds were still asleep in their nests. May be with imagination I could make out slight lightening of the eastern horizon. I finished my tea, wrapped myself in my blanket, and laid back. I closed my eyes, waiting for the morning.

We had hot breakfast at Manmad, and repacked our bedding. The young couple sitting opposite left the train, but no one boarded to replace them. The train was approaching its destination, and was gradually shedding passengers. I bought a news paper and flicked the pages. Rini was in deep conversation with the chemist. I was glad to see that he was more relaxed. I glanced out of the window, only to see brown bare hills, and equally brown and bare fields. Thin cattle were pawing the earth in search of green shoots. Small villages with cluster of huts rushed past from time to time. The landscape was depressing. I closed my eyes in contemplative silence.

The train was on schedule, and we reached Pune at three in the afternoon. The day was pleasantly warm, and a light breeze filtered through the crowded platform. Outside the station building we hired an auto-rickshaw. The driver took us through crowded streets and tree lined boulevards, skirting army barracks keeping the race course to our right. He eventually brought us to the Artificial Limb Centre in the heart of the cantonment area, opposite the Southern Command Hospital with its Malignant Diseases Treatment Centre, and next to the Armed Forces Medical College.

I paid off the auto-rickshaw driver, and walked up to the reception. I handed Col. Ansari's referral letter to the receptionist. We were expected. He gave us a key, and directed us to our rooms. It was a very basic two bedroom self contained accommodation, converted from army barracks. Though utilitarian, the unit had all the essentials for daily living, and arrangements for self catering including gas hobs. It was Monday. The receptionist had asked us to report at the desk at nine o'clock the next morning.

We were met by Subedar Joginder Singh, head of the physiotherapy department. He explained to us that when the limb would become available, he would write to us. He gave us a guided tour of the establishment, and showed us the various stages of progress. Rini was quite fascinated by the variety of appendages. We were taken to the gymnasium, where a few disabled soldiers were working out with their new limbs. At the workshop again we saw how individuals were learning various trades, and gaining dexterity with their new fittings. Physical endurance and retraining of new muscle groups to take on routine coordinated efforts formed a major part of the rehabilitation programme, and included swimming in the on site pool. Camaraderie amongst the rehabilitants at various stages in their rehabilitation helped the beginners to get over the initial despair at the ungainly efforts and the perceived Herculean uphill task. Positive mental attitude and dedication and acceptance of the circumstances are the main strengths necessary for optimum benefit, and camaraderie helps with the diffusion of these qualities into the new comers. Whining and complaining is not encouraged. Most of the men there were soldiers, who sustained shell or mine blast injuries, and had lost an arm, a leg or both. I was moved to see their effort and dedication to develop self sufficiency, and eventually a productive life.

There were very few women, and only those sustaining mine blast injuries in the border areas, or accident victims from Border Roads like Rini were lucky enough to avail this facility. This was totally an army establishment, dedicated to service personnel and their families. Rini was asked to practice a set of exercises to strengthen her quadriceps, and her measurements were taken.

In the evening we strolled along Wanawrie road to Golibar Maidan, and then to the Main street or Mains, as the locals call it. The glitter of the shop fronts was in marked contrast to the sleepy and leafy quiet and forgotten look of the cantonment area, especially the Wanawrie road, which was lined by barbed wire fences that once protected army barracks, now just stand as reminder of the past. The Command Hospital and the Armed Forces Medical Colleges were hidden behind the foliage of tall trees in the fenced off area along either side of the wide road with sparse traffic. At the other end the road passed through a small settlement of hutments at Ram Tekri, a raised hillock with sweeping view of that part of the city. An ancient bridge spanned the trickling waters of a forgotten stream, and winded its way to join the Sholapur road near the Army School of Physical Training. We spent a week in this deceptively rural surroundings, occasionally venturing into the bustling areas of the city like the Deccan Gymkhana, the university near Ganesh Peth, the river turned sewage—The Mulla Mutha, and walked through the sprawling Empress garden. Twice we watched sizzling races with all its excitement at the racecourse. Soon it was time for us to return to Simla and wait for the recall when the limb would be ready. In time we were to know Pune very well indeed, and love it as I have never loved any metropolis ever before; but that had to wait until our next visit.

Rini was getting out of the self-pity mode in company of others who have similar disabilities. She often thought of her childhood, and especially of her mother.

RINI

The cold woke me up: Intense bitter cold. My feet and my nose were icy. I curled my tiny body into a tight ball and pulled the blanket over myself, covering my head and shivered. It was pitch-dark: I stretched out my right hand to locate my mother and snuggled up to her hoping to share her warmth. Eventually I drifted off to deep slumber, waking up to a bright morning. I hated the winter. I can never forget those cold nights.

My earliest childhood recollections consist of a small dark damp room, with a kerosene stove in one corner: Pots, pans, vegetables, containers of condiments, a hand grinder and a knife, scattered around the stove. An old mattress covered the mud-plastered dirt floor of the room in the other corner. A terracotta pot stood against one of the walls. It kept our drinking water cool in the summer months. Our home consisted of that single room made of mud walls, and thatched roof. Water leaked in places when the rains came. My mother tried to catch the drip in an assortment of buckets and utensils. A low opening with a single panel wooden door was the only source of light when it was kept open. Fresh air found its way in through numerous cracks in the construction, standing in the middle of a shantytown: we lovingly called Indira colony after our late Prime Minister.

We used the public toilet across the main road, and if it was busy or too dirty, the open fields at the back of our colony sufficed. The open drain from the public toilet was filthy and smelly. In monsoon, it overflowed, and we had to wade through the filth. We were used to it. It was our home. My mother had to get drinking water from the tube-well at the other end of the colony.

Some of the huts had electricity. They tapped into the overhead cables. This practice was illegal and dangerous. A few even had televisions and refrigerators in their huts. Most of us walked or used the bus, but a few had the luxury of owning scooters. Where we lived, a two wheeler could easily transport the whole family of up to three children.

My mother worked as a cleaner. She spent hours cleaning dirty utensils, dusting and sweeping the houses, and washing dirty clothes. I accompanied her, and sat outside the houses on the veranda. I liked those houses. They had big windows with curtains, nice furniture, electric lights, televisions and cookers. One home even had a big car standing in front of it most of the time. They had their own toilets. My mother did not clean the toilets. Another woman of a lower caste cleaned them. I devised my own games to entertain myself while my mother worked. I talked non-stop when I was with her and she was free, asking her about things that intrigued me. My mother would try to answer as many of my questions as she could, or simply sigh in exasperation and exhaustion.

We had lunch together in one of the houses my mother worked. That meal was part of her salary. In the evenings before going home we visited the market and bought some vegetables. My mother would cook a simple meal. She would laugh with me and sing songs. She had a beautiful voice. Even today, when I am lonely or sad or depressed, her voice rings in my ears. Perhaps those years with my mother were the happiest years of my life. Life then was simple.

One winter evening we were caught in a downpour. Soaking wet, we reached home. My mother lighted the stove to warm us. She dried herself and me and we changed into dry clothes. She could not dry her long hair, and caught a cold. Next few days she had a raging fever and a hacking cough. Our next door neighbour, Akbar, called the doctor. He thought my mother had developed pneumonia, and prescribed her with some antibiotics. He also asked her to get a chest X-ray. My mother could not afford to get a private chest X-ray. She took the antibiotics, and her fever subsided, though the cough persisted.

Months passed, and her cough got gradually worse. A dry hacking cough would rack her, and leave her gasping for breath. She stopped going to work, and asked her friend Rani, who worked in a tailoring shop, to bring her work needing repairs or embroidery as and when extra work became available. She did not get any decent length of sleep at night.

Then one day Rani cajoled her to visit the government hospital and get checked up. The outpatient was very crowded. At last a doctor was free to see her. After a quick examination, he asked her to get a chest X-ray. My mother was diagnosed as having Tuberculosis, and was asked to collect her medicines from the hospital pharmacy every week. Some weeks the hospital pharmacy would run out of stock, and not having enough money to afford two decent meals, my mother economised. She did not buy her medications. Treatment thus was erratic, and there was little improvement.

Since she was told of the diagnosis, she tried to keep me away from her as much as possible. I felt hurt and resentful initially, but soon settled into the routine. She would ask one of our neighbours to take me to work with them, or encourage me to go outside and play with other children.

I liked to go with Bhim. He was a thin middle aged man with greying hair, unshaven stubble and a slight stoop. He was of medium height, and a widower. He usually kept to himself, but was very helpful and caring. He had taken a liking to me; perhaps my loneliness touched a chord with him. I was his princess (Rajkumari). He often came by our place, enquiring after my mother. Sometimes he brought gifts for me—a string of coloured beads, hair curlers, a flute—once he bought me a pair of shiny red shoes. I treasured those shoes, and kept them in their original box. We walked bare feet most of the time, and I did not want my shoes to lose their shine.

Bhim had a pair of pet monkeys. He used to take them to the marketplace, occupy a corner of the pavement, and drum up his "Dumroo" to attract the crowd. He had a resonant voice, which he used well to address the assembled crowd. After enumerating the many qualities his pet monkeys were supposed to possess, he would order them to show some tricks. They would dance, stand on each other's shoulder, and act out the offended wife routine: this act was particularly entertaining and popular with the crowd. The male monkey would try to appease the 'offended' female monkey. Their gesticulations were hilarious, and had the crowd in stitches. The monkeys would go round the crowd at the end of the show, with caps in hands collecting donations.

In the afternoon, when the crowd was thin, Bhim would buy lunch for us, and some nuts and bananas for the monkeys. At dusk we would walk back. If ever I showed any sign of tiredness or complained, Bhim picked me up on his shoulders and carried me home. Despite his thin structure, he was strong.

As sunlight faded and the pink clouds turned to purple, the sky resonated with homeward—bound birds and their impatient chicks. I remember the bright evening star glowing over the telephone masts and electric pylons. On full moon nights, the large pale golden circle hung low in the sky as we trudged home. Bhim would stop just short of our colony at a 'Dhaba'. The owner was his friend. He would order some 'Chhole Bature' for our dinner. By the time I reached home I was invariably half asleep, keeping my eyes open with difficulty. Bhim handed me over to my mother and left to tend to his monkeys. I fell into deep sleep almost immediately.

Rishav had a wooden cart, with four bicycle wheels. The wheels supported a large wooden box, with sliding panels on one side. It also had a canopy like a four poster bed, to protect his mobile kitchen from rain. There was a gas hob and some utensils on the top of the box, along with two tubs with covers, and a drum of drinking water. The drum had a tap to draw water. Inside the box, behind the sliding panels, he kept the gas cylinder, and other odds and ends. A wooden chair was fitted to one end of the box for me to sit as he pushed the cart from the other end. The chair was detachable.

He and his wife cooked two types of curry and put them in the tubs. They prepared some dough, wrapped in moist cloth, and kept it on a wooden plate next to the hob. A wire basket hung from the side of the box containing onions, chillies and eggs. He carried some cooking oil, salt, disposable plates and spoons.

On reaching the desired spot near the town centre, he detached the chair and placed it on the pavement for me to sit. He fried 'bature'

and sold it to hungry passers by. Midday was his busiest period when a brisk business built up. Local shopkeepers and employees queued around his cart. On the whole he was fairly busy and did not have any time to talk to me. He carried a transistor radio blaring out the latest Hindi songs—partly to attract the crowd, and also for my entertainment I thought. I liked to listen to the music, and tried to hum along. I spent my time watching the fascinating stream of people and carts, cars and scooters, buses and rickshaws passing by. I used to play a guessing game to while away the time—like how many cars would come in the next hour, or which make of car will come next and so on. The hustle and bustle of the market place made me oblivious of the passage of time. Very soon it was time to go home. Since Rishav made sure I ate at regular intervals, I was never hungry. Whenever I went out with Rishav I never felt tired, probably because I did not have to walk.

On days when the weather was bad, especially during the monsoon months, Rani took me with her to the dress shop where she worked. She did not have any children of her own. Her husband had left her. She was quite young and very friendly with my mother.

The dress shop was less of a shop, and more like a small-scale garment factory. About ten women worked in a big room under the guidance of its owner. He took orders for various kinds of children's wear. He perhaps made the designs himself. He would make templates and two women would cut different rolls of fabric according to the templates. Rani and the other women then stitched up the pieces and paste motifs to create beautiful dresses. They were all usually very busy except at the lunch break for an hour. The owner frowned upon talking and gossiping at work.

This shop was in a quiet part of the town. The room was of fair size with a few sewing machines and a long table. It was brightly lit and cool. The owner lived upstairs. Before Diwali, Id or Christmas, the shop took on a different character. Piles of fabric were scattered everywhere, the owner became tense and shouted at the workers. Monotonous rattling of the sewing machines was the only sound most of the time. Everyone was bent over and concentrated on their work, with customary breaks often forgotten. They had deadlines to meet.

Rani usually gave me a piece of fabric and a pair of scissors to design clothes for my dolls. I would be happily cutting and shaping for hours. Sometimes I fell asleep on the mat, and Rani would wake me up when it was time to go home. Everyone, including the owner was kind to me, and gave me presents from time to time. I had my special corner in the room, where I worked hard at creating dresses to clothe the little people of my imagination. I brought the pieces home, and my mother would stitch them up. I often showed them off proudly to anyone who had time to listen to me. When they became dirty, my mother would throw them away, telling me that they had become old fashioned.

On our way back home from Rani's place of work she often lingered at various shops, bought some grocery for herself and my mother, saving her the trouble of walking all this way in her weakened condition. After dinner, Rani sat with my mother to chat. I fell asleep listening to the murmur of their voices, once in a while broken with peals of laughter and my mother's cough.

Akbar had a vegetable stall in the open market. He got up very early in the morning, even before the birds left their nests. In the semidarkness he rode his bicycle to the whole sellers. There he spent time selecting and buying fresh vegetables of all kinds. He loaded jute bags full of fresh vegetables onto the back of the hired pick-up van, and the driver would deliver it at the market. Shaheen would be there to unload the van at Akbar's stall. She would also carry an aluminium container full of chapati or paratha, pickles and some curry for Akbar's breakfast, and later for his lunch. Once Akbar reached his stall, he would lock his bike, spread jute bags and tarpaulins on the dirt floor. Sort the vegetables and put them in woven baskets made from bamboo strips, to display his wares strategically in an attempt to attract potential buyers. Shaheen would go back home to tend to the routine housework.

Sometimes Shaheen took me to the market with her. The bustling crowd and the noise fascinated me, as did the blend of myriad smell: condiments, fish, flowers, sweat and incense sticks. Often it was difficult to distinguish any word in the cacophony of raised tempers: haggling customers and vendors making their sales pitch to attract customers. There would be shouting, jostling, haggling, angry voices, and pleading notes and a general hum of excitement and human activity. The fishmongers and the butchers were adjacent to the green grocers. Business was brisk and tempers frayed.

Akbar had a couple of cushions to sit on, and a pair of scales in front of him to weigh the vegetables. A pile of measuring weights lay in front of him. They did not have any money box or till. All notes and coins were kept under a jute bag, accessing it by lifting a corner of the bag.

Akbar would stand from time to time and shout out his bargain prices, trying to attract customers whenever the flow of buyers waned. The hustle and bustle kept him busy all morning. Both he and Shaheen attended to the customers. I sat in a corner behind them, watched and wondered at the medley of humanity and range of emotions. After a lull at midday, business would pick up pace in the late afternoon and evening, when commuters, on their way back from work would come looking for essentials and bargains. Vendors would also be more liberal in their haggling, knowing that whatever was not sold would go waste.

At the end of the day, after darkness had settled, Akbar and Shaheen would count the money, put it in a wallet, load the unsold vegetables in jute bags and sling the bags on either side of the rear seat of his bicycle. He would let me sit on the frame in front of his seat in side saddle fashion. I had to hold the handle rod tightly in the middle to keep my balance. He would push the bike, and Shaheen would follow. While dropping me off he would give some of the unsold vegetables to my mother, and keep the rest for their own consumption.

Our colony had about two hundred huts. Quite a large number of residents were single. Salim was in his twenty third year. He was handsome and shy. He was a cobbler by trade and I saw him often sitting on the pavement near the market with his shoe-shine box in front of him, and assortment of tools and nails by his side. He repaired foot-wear and polished shoes. He always appeared to be very busy, leaning over concentrating on his work. Whenever he saw me, he would greet me, and give me a toffee of which he seemed to have an inexhaustible supply.

Kali was a rotund man with a happy face, always breaking into a smile. He owned a sweet meat shop in the market. I had to pass the shop when ever I went with Shaheen. Kali was about forty. From conversations overheard, I knew he had taken a large bank loan to open his shop. He employed two assistants. They made various kinds of sweet meat and 'samosas', 'kachouris' etc. I was always fascinated by the way they made 'Jalebis', the intricate curls and designs. His wife stayed at home looking after the two children they had. I heard his shop was doing well, and soon he would be able to buy a home in town.

A few of the residents, who had regular jobs as bank clerks or working in the municipal office, were snobbish. Subodh was one of them. He and his wife did not mix with most of the other residents and shielded their children from the 'bad influence' of the local children. Subodh was very punctual, and stuck slavishly to a routine. Bhim once joked that you could set your watch by Subodh's routine. I suppose Subodh did not earn much, and could not afford a house in the town yet he looked down upon the poorer residents. His children went to the local missionary school in their starched uniform.

Bishu was nearing retirement. He had been a postman most of his life. He rode his bicycle to the main post office, collected the letters to be distributed in his area, and diligently did his job. Twice a day the mail came, whatever the weather. Bishu made sure that residents in his area of distribution got their letters in time. He was a kindly man, and with all the tips he received during the festive months, he used to buy gifts for us, the children. He was well liked by all.

Akram was another young man who lived alone. He was a welder and worked in a factory. He was very serious, and whenever he was at home, he was engrossed in his books. When I asked him what he was reading, he smiled and replied that he was preparing to become an engineer. Now I realise that he must have been studying for a diploma. Akram was also a health fanatic. He would jog in the morning before going to work, and exercise at home with some weights. He was a loner, and did not socialise much. May be he did not have much free time to socialise. He had bought a new Bajaj scooter, and gave us kids a whirl in it from time to time. We liked it. He said he bought it to save time commuting to work.

Mansoor was enterprising. He was a graduate, but could not get any job. He took a bank loan and bought an auto-rickshaw. An auto-rickshaw has the engine of a scooter, but the rear of the chassis is widened and supported on two wheels to seat three comfortably. In practice up to seven passengers are crammed into it for short commutes. No other vehicle, other than two wheelers can match an auto-rickshaw when it comes to negotiating traffic or narrow lanes in the rush hour. It is the most convenient and economical and efficient mode of travel in any Indian town. Mansoor was flamboyant and was sure to be the centre of any gathering. He was a lady's man.

Our colony had its rougher elements too. One morning I heard that fifteen men were rushed to hospital in critical condition after drinking cheap liquor. At the time I wondered why anyone would want to drink poison, but now I realise it was cheap liquor adulterated with methylated spirit. Ten of the fifteen died, and the others were blinded for life.

A group of youths terrorised businesses across the street, and asked for protection money. Protection from whom, I wondered. Police turned a blind eye to their criminal activities. In fact there was hardly any police presence near our colony. Then of course there were a group of young women who lived on the other side of the colony, near the main road. They did not seem to do any work but lived well, wore nice clothes and jewellery. Their huts had electricity, refrigerators and table fans. They received lots of visitors in the evenings, arriving in cars and taxis. They also had good wooden furniture. I sometimes asked my mother how they could afford to live so well. My mother replied that they had rich friends. Often at night when I woke up, I could hear drunken laughter and screams from that part of our colony. I sometimes felt scared.

One day my mother told me that I was old enough to go to school. There were two schools near us. One was the government school, and Christian Missionaries ran the other. The government school was free, and did not have any school uniform. My mother enrolled me in the government school, and Shaheen's younger daughter gave me her old books. I was very proud to be going to school, and told everyone I met. My mother combed my hair, and tied a pony tail with a coloured ribbon. Junior school was provided with hot free meals at lunch. By the end of the first day I was tired, and went off to bed early.

Over the next few months I learnt to write simple words and do sums. We learnt rhymes and had to read in class. Best of all I enjoyed spending break times playing with my friends, and making as much noise as possible. In class though, we had to be quiet and attentive. Every evening when I reached home, I would proudly display my newly acquired knowledge and even correct my mother if she appeared to be making mistakes.

That winter my mother's cough got worse. She looked thinner, and appeared to have lost weight. She would tire easily and become a little irritable. Her cough would not allow her to sing any more, and in the evenings she would ask me to sing to her the songs she had taught me. She would hold me tightly and kiss my forehead. One morning I was woken up by her fit of coughing, and noticed that she was coughing blood on the piece of cloth she was holding over her mouth. It scared me. I asked her if she was all right, and she reassured me. I was not convinced. Later that day I told Rani what happened. She came home with me and quizzed my mother. They had an argument. Rani was angry with my mother, who appeared very calm and serene.

"What will be, will be," my mother said to Rani, who burst out in tears and left our house. I was left puzzled by this exchange of words.

My mother got steadily worse, and gradually became so weak that she could not stand on her own. Rani and Shaheen came regularly to look after us, feed us and nurse my mother. I woke up to a quiet morning one day. I realised something was different, and then I noticed that my mother was not coughing any more. I tried to wake her up but she did not respond. She felt cold. I was scared, and ran to Rani for help. She held me in her arms. She was crying. She asked me to stay at her place, and walked out. Later when she returned, she was pale and had been crying. She held me and told me that my mother had died; that she had gone to heaven, and may be she will become one of the stars. I was quiet. Death was not new to me. Living amongst the poorest people where free health care was almost non-existent, I have seen people die in our colony—but my mother! I did not expect to lose her. I realised then that I was truly alone in the world. I wondered who would look after me now.

Akbar came and gave me the little jewellery my mother had, and my clothes. They had burnt the mattress and thrown away the utensils. Bhim, Bishu, Kali and some other residents of our colony took my mother's body to the crematorium. I accompanied them. After the body was cremated, they threw the ashes in the Ganges.

I did not cry that night. I had lost my tears. I was stunned. Rani forced me to eat a few mouthfuls of rice. I ate automatically. Rani took leave from her work, and tried to encourage me into my daily routine. I would go to school and come back, but I stopped smiling and I stopped playing. I stayed with Rani for a few weeks. I saw a new family move into our shack. There was no change in me. Rani got worried. After discussing with Bhim, Akbar and Rishav, she decided that I should be removed from that place, to somewhere, where I would not be reminded of my mother day in and day out. The question was where! Ultimately it was Bhim who said that he would take me to the orphanage in Dehradoon run by Catholic nuns.

Next morning everyone bade farewell to me. Bhim took me to the railway station, and for the first time in my life, I boarded a train. I was seven that winter. I had a small bag with all my worldly possessions—a few dresses and my doll and my mother's jewellery. I did not know what I was getting into, where I was going. I trusted Bhim. Did I have a choice?

The uncertainties of my future was causing me some apprehension, but being so young, I did not realise the full implications. The monotonous clanging of the steel against steel lulled my senses, and I drifted in and out of fitful slumber. Whenever I opened my eyes, trees and farms and cattle and hills rushed past my window, taking me far away from the world I grew up in, the world I knew. Finally putting my head on Bhim's lap I slept through the rest of the journey. I woke up by the sudden jerk as the train pulled into a station and stopped.

Vendors and porters and passengers were shouting. It was impossible to separate voices from the din and confusion on the platform. People were getting in and out of the train. We climbed down from our carriage. I was clutching my small possession. I was amazed at the sea of faces, rush of feet and the push of the crowd. Bhim guided me away from the bedlam. I heard the guard blowing his whistle, and saw green flags being waved. The train chugged ponderously out of the station, gradually picking speed. Smiling and tearful faces at the windows waving frantically at friends and relations they were leaving behind.

It was quite late. The station was brightly lit with neon lights. I was feeling hungry. Bhim asked me to go to the toilet and refresh myself. When I met him again, he had washed himself, and combed his hair. We walked down to the railway restaurant and ordered some food. After dinner we walked down to the crowded ticket hall, and found an unoccupied corner floor space. We lay down to sleep. I was used to the mosquitoes, but the bright light, noise and the unfamiliar surroundings made it difficult to sleep. I closed my eyes, and the tiredness of the journey helped me to drift into oblivion. The next thing I knew was Bhim shaking me. It was morning. I washed, and cleaned my teeth with my finger, had something to eat and set off for the orphanage.

A policeman directed us. It was not far from the railway station, and we walked. The day was bright and sunny, with a pleasant breeze. The town was coming to life, and there was a fair bit of traffic on the roads. Pedestrians jostled to reach bus stops, offices or other destinations. Everyone seemed to be in a hurry. I was looking around with wondering eyes, and taking in all the sights and sounds of this new town. We passed a chapel and a school and then Bhim turned into the driveway of an old building that looked like a hostel. He knocked on the door, and a young nun opened it. Bhim asked to see the person in charge. We were escorted to the office, and asked to wait there. She disappeared inside.

Presently she came back accompanied by an older nun, whom I later came to know as 'Mother Superior'. Bhim must have told her about me because she did not ask me anything except my name, and after some pleasantries she asked the young nun to take me upstairs. Bhim gave me a tight hug, and wiping his eyes bade me farewell and left. I was crying. At the time I did not know that I'd never see Bhim again.

The young nun introduced herself as Christine, and asked me to follow her. She took me to the dormitory. No one was there, but there were two rows of single beds and some bedside lockers. She took me to a bedside locker and told me to put my belongings in it. She informed me that we were in the girls' dormitory, and there were forty girls of various ages in residence at the time. The youngest was six years old, and the oldest sixteen. I later learnt that girls over the age of sixteen were encouraged to look for employment, and leave the orphanage.

She asked me to take a shower, clean myself and get into clean clothes. She gave me a clean towel, and showed me how the shower worked. She watched me for a minute, and then taking a cake of soap, started to lather me. She scrubbed me so hard, that my skin started to sting. I whimpered, but was asked to keep quiet and allow her to get rid of the dirt. The water was cold and I shivered. I tried to wriggle out, but she had a firm grip on my right upper arm. She washed all the soap off, and in the process got wet herself and that made me laugh. She scrubbed me dry with the towel, and asked me to wear the cleanest dress I had. She brushed my hair, pulling it back and pleated it into a single braid. She took me to the kitchen, and gave me some food. She explained that all the other children were at school at the time, and that I would meet them presently.

Christine, or Sister Roberts as I learnt later she was formally addressed, gave me a guided tour of the building and its grounds. There was a large hall each in the first and second floors, both were being used as dormitories. There were shower rooms and toilets on each of these floors. Ground floor consisted of kitchen, utility and dining rooms, offices and a common room with a grand piano sitting in one corner of the room. There were scattered sofas and coffee tables in small clusters around the room. There was one black and white television in one corner. This room had two big windows, with floral curtains tied back with braided tassels. The room had wooden floor, glistening from regular mopping and polishing. The nuns lived in a house behind this building, secluded and hidden behind a wall of hedges, creepers and tall trees. There was a bit of open ground between the orphanage and the school, and again some more open space between the school and the chapel. These open grounds were used as playgrounds during term times.

By the end of the tour I was feeling quite hungry and tired. I was no longer as scared or sad as when I said goodbye to Bhim. The optimism of youth and Christine's friendly approach had calmed my uncertainties. I was looking forward to meeting the other children. I am gregarious by nature, and like to be with people. I can mix with strangers quite easily.

The regimented life of the orphanage was in sharp contrast to what I was used to. Time had no meaning in the colony, except when I was in school. Here every activity was timed. The time we left our beds, morning exercises, breakfast, school, lunch break, homework time, dinner, washing up and lights off were all predetermined. Life was clock-watching. On Sundays we had to sweep and clean the orphanage, wash our clothes, attend mass, help with gardening, and occasionally went on outings under supervision, especially in the afternoons. The Sunday evening was the only time we had to ourselves. Christine had noticed that I liked to sing, and could sing in tune. She had taken me under her wing to train my voice. Thus I spent most Sunday evenings either in front of the grand piano singing, or sitting behind it and playing the keys. Christine taught me the basics of voice training and initiated me to western classical music.

As I grew older, I had to help with the cooking and washing dishes, take charge of younger girls and help them with their work. Occasionally I was allowed to play the church organ on Sundays. I was not a Christian, but attending mass was part of our routine. I enjoyed singing in the choir. School work was proving more and more difficult, especially maths. I liked languages and history. I grew used to the orphanage life, and accepted it as my home.

We had very little worries and no practical knowledge or experience of the outside world. We learnt about world events through the radio and television and newspapers. The social upheavals and communal riots outside our gates did not touch us. Thus it was a shock and a devastating blow to my sense of security and well-being, when mother superior told us one morning in the assembly that due to financial difficulties faced by the church, it was decided to close down this orphanage. Younger children would be transferred to a different orphanage in another town, while older teenagers would have to look for suitable employment and positions to support themselves. We had only three months to look for a livelihood. The full implication of her words took time to sink in, and again I was scared.

Mother superior and other nuns helped us collect newspaper cuttings of job advertisements. We soon found that either we were too young, or too inexperienced or unqualified for most jobs. After being unsuccessful at our attempts for two months, we were getting desperate. One day on my way back from one of the interviews, I noticed a small queue of young men and women near an army barrack in the cantonment area. On enquiring I found that the Border Roads Organisation was recruiting manual labourers. The minimum age was eighteen years. I was sixteen, but big for my age and passed myself off as eighteen.

I had never heard of Border Roads, and did not know what they did. All I gathered was that it was a government institution, linked to the armed forces. I did not know what was expected of me, but was desperate to get a paying job, any job that the nuns would approve. I joined the queue. Most of the applicants appeared very poor and illiterate. There were people of all ages. I noticed that they were selecting only the young and strong. The recruiting officer did warn me that I was expected to do heavy lifting and work for long hours. He quoted an hourly rate of pay, which did not make much sense to me. Having lived a sheltered life, I was not aware of cost of living. Those selected were asked to report there the next morning. He told us that we will be based at Joshimath, about a hundred kilometres from our town and at a height of about 6000 feet. He asked us to take warm clothes and blankets with us.

That evening I spoke to mother superior and the other nuns after dinner, and told them of the offer. They were not very happy, and did not want me to start my life as a manual labourer. When I pointed out to them that with my qualifications and age I did not have much choice, they relented with reluctance. I had to promise them that I would save up, and get back to formal education as soon as I could. I could see in their eyes that they were worried about me, but we had very little choice. Time was running out.

THE HERMIT

I could hear murmur of voices. I was not sure where I was, but was aware of a pounding in my head and a severe headache. I felt my head was about to split. I opened my eyes, and had to shut them promptly. The glare was too intense, and seared through my brain. It worsened my headache. I tried to remember what happened. I came up with a blank. I could not remember my name or who I was. I kept my eyes tightly shut, and must have dozed off.

I opened my eyes again much later. The room was in darkness except for a single oil lamp, breaching the darkness, creating a shadowy gloom. A voice near me spoke:

"Ah! You are awake at last."

I looked towards the voice, and saw an ancient face creased with lines, a pair of black twinkling eyes, and the lower half of the face covered with a snowy flowing beard. I tried to move my head, but the sharp pain made me wince.

"Stay still," said the voice, "You are still running a temperature." He paused, and then asked "Are you thirsty?"

I felt parched, and had difficulty in swallowing. I nodded. He lifted and supported my head, and held a glass of water to my lips. I drank and drained the glass in one breath. He eased my head back on the pillow. I realised that I was lying on a thin mattress on the floor of a small room. I could not see the walls, since the meagre light from the oil lamp failed to penetrate the darkness far enough to illuminate them.

"Try and rest as much as you can." The voice advised. "You are still very weak and fevered. You need to get your strength back."

I had no desire to move, and taking his advice, shut my eyes and drifted off to a troubled sleep. I woke up in the middle of the night drenched in sweat, and shivering with cold. I lay awake for sometime, pulled a blanket tightly around myself, and curling up on my side went back to sleep. I have no recollection of how many days I spent in that Trance like sleep, occasionally opening my eyes, drinking, and more lately eating nuts and fruits and raisins before drifting back to oblivion. Whenever I opened my eyes, the kindly ancient face seemed to hover around nearby always, speaking gently to me. Then one day I woke up early in the morning, and noticed a thin covering of snow on the hills that I could see through the open door. I had looked around and found myself in a small room, twelve feet by ten feet. I was lying against one of the walls on a thin mattress, and hugging a couple of blankets to preserve body heat. The Sun was shining on the distant snow covered peaks, but the hills outside my door were still in the shade. The small rectangular sky visible to me was blue with a few streaking cirrus clouds. I could hear chirping of birds, and the roar of a waterfall.

The room was bare of any furniture. A sitting mat was placed on the other side of the room, with a few pictures hanging low on that wall. A wooden platform held a few statues. Next to the platform was a tall book-shelf, dominating the room. It contained many thick volumes. A narrow doorway led to another room, but I could not see inside that room due to the angle of my visual field. My head was not aching any more, nor were my eyes burning when I opened them. I craned my neck to get a better view and lifted myself on one elbow. My muscles ached, and I still felt very weak.

The doorway was filled with the elderly man coming back. His wet hair was splayed over his shoulders. Droplets of water clung to his torso. A white loin cloth was wrapped around his waist. He was wearing wooden sandals.

"How are you feeling today?" He smiled at me and asked.

"Much better thank you." I replied.

"I think you are strong enough today to leave your bed. Come let me help you. I want you to take a few steps, and wash your face if you can." He said.

I stood up with his help, swayed a little with dizziness, but recovered. I walked outside and sat on a wooden bench. I felt as though I had no strength left in me, and it was an effort to control my legs, even to put them one in front of the other. Taking my time, and with help I managed to negotiate the few stone steps that took me to the river's edge. I stooped and scooped up a jug of water. I splashed water on my face, and gurgled and cleaned my teeth with my finger. The cold water felt refreshing and revitalising on my skin.

"Don't fall off the ledge," He warned me. "The river is deep and the current is strong here."

When I had finished, he helped me up the steps to his cottage. I sat down on the wooden bench, exhausted. He gave me some fruits, dates and raisins to eat, and brewed me a cup of hot sweet white tea.

He sat next to me on the bench and asked, "Who are you?"

I pondered over the question, and to my horror I could not find the answer. I could not remember anything of my past, beyond the few tortured days of sickness spent in this cottage.

"I do not know," I said. "I cannot remember anything before coming here."

He nodded his head in understanding. "I am Anand," He said. "That is not the name my parents gave me. When I renounced the materialistic world, I had to choose a different name."

He waited for my response, and when none was forthcoming, he said," I found you by the river one morning, about a month ago. You were half drowned, battered and badly bruised. I do not think you had any broken bones, but from your injuries I assumed you were dead, and then you moved. I took you up to my hermitage with help. Your recovery was rather stormy. You developed pneumonia, probably from exposure and took your time getting better. I am surprised that you managed to pull through. You are a prime example of the saying "If God desires you to live, nothing can destroy you."

"I have to call you by some name, what about Amar, meaning someone who never dies?"

I shrugged my shoulders, "I don't think that's my name. It does not ring a bell, but then 'What's in a name.' I have nothing against Amar, and I don't mind being called by that name." I felt tired, went back to my bed and slept. I ate in the afternoon and slept again. I gradually got my strength back. It was almost a month since I was renamed, that I could say that I felt strong again.

One day I asked Anand why he kept his book collection, very few of them had anything to do with theology. He had the Vedas, Upanishads, Bhagwat Gita, Holy Bible and the Quoran, but the other books were on as diverse subjects as economics, political science, physics, mathematics, world history, corporate law, astrology and biographies.

"I was an economist, and held a senior position in the Reserve bank of India before I became a 'Sadhu'. These were subjects I liked to dabble in as a hobby, and I still do, though more and more of my time now-a-days is spent on meditation. From time to time I browse through these books. I subscribe to one of the economic journals, and occasionally write articles that get published. These books provide me with food for thought."

"What made you give up your position and the life of comfort to come here and become a hermit?"

I asked.

"It is a long story," He said. "I'll tell you later. How are you feeling today? Do you think you can come with me for a short walk?"

"I'll give it a try," I said.

We set off on a rocky path, following the stream flowing in front of the hermitage. He walked leisurely, giving me time to catch up. We came up to the confluence of two rivers, one with muddy water, and the other blue water of the melted ice. We were standing about twenty metres above the water level.

"This is Dev Prayag," Anand said. The two rivers you see are Alaknanda and Bhagirathi. They merge here to form the Ganges. You know, the Ganges is called the holy river not only because it irrigates the plains of Northern and Eastern India, but also it has the inherent capacity to neutralise pollutants much more quickly than other rivers. Looking at the two narrow strips of water from here, it is difficult to visualise the two thousand and five hundred kilometres long course, at places so wide that standing on one bank you cannot see the opposite bank: more so in the monsoon, when the flood waters spread over miles upon miles of fertile land, submerging villages and forests."

"For more than two millennia we have neglected and abused the river, dumping all rubbish and refuse and dead bodies into its waters. Even the great capacity of self purification of this holy river is struggling to survive with the present load of effluents. At places the river is practically running raw sewage. At long last the government is trying to curb river pollution, and setting up sewage treatment plants along her banks. Centuries of habit die hard. Villagers still bathe and water their animals in the river. I am optimistic that in time despite the huge demands on the river, it will survive, and run fresh and clean and life giving water from the Himalayas to the Bay of Bengal."

"In order to combat floods in the North and draught in the South, planners had come up with a viable plan of canals and dams joining all the major rivers, and diverting the excess water in to canals to feed the draught prone regions. Unfortunately, some of our neighbouring countries fear that they may be cut off from their source of water in the summer months, and oppose the plan. It is a pity, because Bangladesh is deluged with floods every year with massive loss of life, crops and property, sometimes covering as much as three quarters of that county. The floods usher in diseases and famine amongst the poorest, and many perish while others languish in poverty."

We sat on a stone bench, facing the confluence and the deep gorges. The township lay sprawled on the left bank. The hills are less steep on that side, and beyond the township the slopes are cut into steps for cultivation. We could see people going about their business, buses and cars moving along the road. It was a cold December day, with a slight breeze and a bright Sun, fending off waves of clouds trying to eclipse it. I wrapped the blanket more tightly around my shoulders. Anand was not wearing anything other than his loin cloth.

"Don't you feel cold?" I remarked.

"You get used to it," Was his reply. I had my doubts. I did not think I could ever get so used to cold that I could shed my clothes.

"Come on, let's get back. You must be hungry," Anand said.

I got up to my feet, and slid my feet into the wooden sandals. I had become quite used to them. Considering that today was the first time I ventured far from the hermitage, I was pleased with my performance, though I was feeling exhausted.

"You take rest while I make some food," Anand said when we reached his hermitage.

I did not need to be told twice. I stretched my mattress and lay on my back, pulling the blanket over my body, and closing my eyes. I often wondered at moments like this, with my eyes closed, and in half asleep and half-awake state, who was I? Where did I come from! Anand thought that I was probably a tourist, who fell off a cliff into the river, and was washed down. He did not expect me to have lost my memory. He has been philosophical, and asked me to be patient, until my memory recovers. At times I wondered if it will ever recover, if I will ever know who I was.

After dinner we sat on a stone step outside. I wrapped a thick blanket around myself. Anand started asking me random questions on science, biology, commerce and literature.

"You have had some education obviously, but I am not sure to what level." He said at last. "I think I'll try to improve your knowledge and language skills. We shall discuss and debate issues as they come up. That way your mind will remain sharp and you will learn to present your thoughts in a coherent orderly manner. An orderly mind is of great help in decision making."

Thus began our evening ritual of educational sessions. We had no set pattern or subject, the emphasis was on languages, maths and economics. We discussed various topics, including Indian history, mythology, geo-politics and world trade I learnt the concept of supply and demand: if there is no demand, unemployment goes up, and if there is more demand inflation sets in. I learnt the use of government taxes as a source of revenue, and also a method of controlling demand. I was told about money supply, relationship between salary and cost of living, consumerism and artificially increased demand for manufacturing to survive. I learnt about assets and equity, loan and gearing. He introduced me to the fascinating world of economics and commerce.

Almost three months had passed since my accident. I was no nearer to solving the problem of my identity. I adopted Anand's routine of getting up at dawn, wash and bathe in the icy waters of the Ganges, spend an hour on Yoga, and then have some fruits and milk for breakfast. Anand would sit in meditation for hours, while I either went for a walk if the weather was good, or browse through the books on the shelf. I liked to read the autobiographies: Swami Vivekananda, Gandhi, Mark Twain, Tolstoy, Plutarch, Napoleon, Churchill etc. These books opened my eyes to complexity of the human nature and its greatness. This austere routine was helping me to get stronger, and I started to feel full of life and vitality again. Usually after a frugal lunch Anand would instruct me in one of his pet subjects and set some tasks for me. We went for a walk in the evenings, continuing our discussion on the subject and continue in that vein until I was ready for bed, and drifted off to sleep. Anand would immerse himself into deep meditation till late at night. I do not know if he actually slept or not.

The weather was getting better. Cherries and apricots and apples were in bloom all around us. Blossom in the hills is colourful and pretty, with coloured petals drifting in the breeze, giving the impression of snowfall in bright sunshine. The temperature became milder during the day. The water level in the river rose with augmentation of water flow from melting snow high up in the Himalayas.

"What do you want to do with your life?" Anand asked me one day.

"I haven't thought of it much since the accident," I said. "Why can't I just stay in these hills like you? It is very calm and peaceful here."

"Everything in life has its rhythm and time. The usual cycle of life starts off in childhood, followed by that of the student (Brmhacharya), that celibate and austere phase of life when you try to glean knowledge. Then you grow to take risks as the soldier or entrepreneur, maturing to a family man, a civic leader and eventually retirement. After the age of fifty, when you have achieved most of your potentials, you can decide to come back into these hills to meditate, and seek salvation. Only after you have fulfilled your duties may you come back for the peace and tranquillity. You will then have the maturity of understanding nature and Divinity. Thousands of years ago our ancestors practised this rhythm of life. If you read the mythologies, Ramayana or Mahabharata you will find that even the kings and queens left their palaces to go into the forest to lead the austere life of a hermit, to meditate and be one with nature. They wanted to be away from the distractions of power and wealth."

"Your time has not come. Stay with me for now, but later this year you will have to go back into society to fulfil your potentials. Life is but a journey where you learn to live. You must do your duty as you see it without any expectation of reward or gratitude. That way you will lead a happy fulfilling life. It is the expectations of reward or gratitude that bring sadness and frustration when they are not met."

"You did not tell me why you chose this life over the comforts and luxury of wealth?" I asked.

Anand was quiet for a few minutes, and then he said, "Come, let's sit down on the steps from where we can see the high snow covered peaks of Kamet and Nandadevi."

A deep blue sky with cotton wool balls of white cloud over a sunbathed landscape of fast flowing rivers and deep gorges met our eyes as we came out. The white peaks looked so close, high up, towering over the green fringes of the hill tops. We sat down on the steps facing the mountains.

"I am in my eighties now," He said. "It happened a long time ago. I was a senior executive in the Reserve Bank of India and was staying in New Delhi. My wife and I were quite contented with life. Our son was in the final year of his medical college. He wanted to become a surgeon. Our daughter had followed in my footsteps and completed a master's degree in economics. She was working on her PhD. She was twenty-three, and was very pretty, witty and lively. She had an active social life. Her friends were in and out of our home all the time. We thought it was time to get her married, and settled in life. We did not want our daughter to give up her carrier, or move too far away from us."

"A young man had joined in our department a couple of years ago, and showed a lot of promise. He was smart, well behaved, intelligent, articulate, competent, confident and polite. He had a very good academic record. He specialised in the development of micro-economy. I was impressed with his work. His parents lived in Bombay. His father was a business man, and owned a small company manufacturing motor parts, that he exported. He had two brothers, one of whom had joined his father after doing a degree in mechanical engineering from Indian Institute of Technology in Bombay."

"One evening I invited him to dinner at home, and introduced him to my daughter. They liked each other, and started going out. I gave them six months, and then asked them if they wished to marry. They agreed. I wrote to the boy's father, and he invited us to Bombay to get to know each other."

"It was May, and my son was back from his hostel on summer vacation. I booked seats in Indian airlines, and we were ready to go to Bombay. Unexpectedly, that week the OPEC raised the price of oil, and the world economy took a downward turn. There was severe pressure on the rupee for devaluation. I had to stay back. I told my wife to go with our children and future son in law to Bombay, and that I would join them within a day or two. I rang Bombay to let them know of the changed plan."

"The day they were to fly, I was snowed under with paper work and cabinet meetings that I had to brief. I reached back home at eleven that evening. I already had a working dinner, and was not hungry. I changed into my sleeping suit, and switched on the television to catch the news headlines. The national news was nearly finished. The news reader was repeating the headlines. I was not paying close attention initially, but then I saw the wreckage of an Indian airlines aircraft, and heard her saying 'IA flight 323 from New Delhi to Bombay was blown up today in mid air by a bomb. A terrorist group has claimed responsibility. There were no survivors.' I was transfixed to my seat, and could not move for some time. I hoped it was a different flight. I rang the airport to confirm. I dressed quickly and drove like a madman to the domestic airport to check the passenger list. Their names were swimming in front of my eyes on the list, as I started to cry. I controlled myself quickly, and came back to our empty house. The next few days passed in a blur. I do not remember much. Once the remains were cremated and religious ceremonies were over, I took a month's leave and went to Gangotri. I was very depressed those days and for once in my life I did not know what to do. I met a sadhu who took one look at me, and told me I was ready for a change in life. I did not understand him. He became more explicit."

"Life is a lonely journey for each soul. Parents, wife, sons and daughters, they are nothing but illusions. The gamut of emotions that we experience in our lifetime is of our own creation. During our lifetime we are tested with situations beyond our control. The more you get mired in the emotional quicksand, the worse illusions you will suffer. You must learn to control your senses and your emotions. Once you have achieved complete mastery over your emotions, you stop feeling happy or sad, pain or elation. Your life's journey reaches its end and you merge with the Supreme Power we call God. Some souls have to be reborn again and again, to suffer through the illusions before they achieve mastery over their emotions."

"That day I did not quite understand the meaning of his words, but today, after years spent in meditation and soul searching I do understand. You cannot be sad if you don't feel the loss, you cannot be happy if you don't feel pleasure. Seasons change in their own time at a given rhythm. The tree is neither sad to lose its leaves in winter, nor happy to gain new foliage in the spring. Once you achieve inner peace, emotions will never again take you on the roller coaster journey."

Anand paused. There was not much for me to say. I was going over his words, and trying to fathom its meaning. We had been sitting on the stone steps for a while, and the Sun was already well over to the West.

"Come, let's go for a walk," Anand said. I followed him in silence, musing over the unpredictability and fragility of our life.

As the Sun hid behind the mountain ranges, there was a perceptible drop in the ambient temperature. The breeze stirred restless leaves, tugging at them and tearing the dried and brown ones from their anchoring stem, into the eddies, dancing around us as we ambled along the well trodden path down to the edge of the water. The rustling noise was steadily being replaced, and then drowned by the splashes and murmur and gurgling of the mountain river.

There were people around us. Some were out to enjoy the delightful evening, others rushing back from work. Some women were returning after collecting drinking water from the river, delicately balancing the earthenware pots on their heads, glancing our way as we passed them. Some saluted Anand in the traditional way and Anand returned their salutation. Others tried to engage him in conversation. Most people appeared to know him, respect him. By the time we returned back to the hermitage, I was exhausted. I realised how much toll the recent illness had taken off me.

We got into a routine. Anand would wake me up early in the morning, well before Sunrise. We would go down to the river and wash and bathe in the cold water. Coming back, I'll prepare breakfast for myself and read, while Anand would meditate until late morning. We would discuss and debate whatever I had read that morning, with a short interruption for midday meals. Anand tried to teach me the subjects he knew best, and pass on to me distillate of his years of experience. Sometimes I could grasp his meaning, at other times he left me scratching my head. By late afternoon we would go for a long walk, often climbing to the top of the hill, and enjoy the rolling vista of the foothills as it dropped away to merge with the plains at the limit of our vision. We would sit on the stones, lapping in the beauty and tranquillity. Anand often submerged into deep meditation, rousing himself well after darkness had set in. He seemed to know every inch of the mountainside, and would lead me unhesitatingly and unerringly through the darkness back to our abode. I went to sleep soon after dinner, but I think Anand busied himself with writing journal articles, his diary or manuscripts in the dim light of the oil lamp, and meditation.

I was regaining my strength quickly. I was learning mathematics, economics, English, Sanskrit and philosophy. There was no syllabus or timetable. I would pick up a topic to read, and later Anand would dissect my knowledge, encourage me to debate the issues and come to my own conclusions. Just like the soft and elusive dusk, knowledge has no boundaries. Interpretations and applications depend entirely on the pupil.

The weather turned for the worse. Rain and snow lashed the mountains, cold winds howled down the gorges, whistling through trees, whipping their branches in a frenzied dance. Snow sleet and blustery wind increased the wind chill factor. Wet tracks with icy films and liquid mud made walking down to the river quite treacherous, and I often found my feet running ahead of me, forcing me to massage my traumatised nether end. We had to stop our evening walks, and were confined to our quarters most of the day. Anand took this opportunity to concentrate on my education, teaching me the mysteries of supply and demand, vagaries of the stock market, gearing and hostile take-overs, venture capitalists and bankruptcy. I also learnt the principles of Vedic Mathematics, where complex mathematical problems can be solved mentally and swiftly. Anand helped me to polish my English and presentation skills. I also learnt yoga and the art of meditation.

The three months from March to May was spent in close proximity of each other. We learnt a lot about each other. We became very close. Since I did not know who I was, Anand took the place of my father and I his foster son, or may be a teacher and his disciple described us better. Anand's style of educating me in his subjects mesmerised me and increased my thirst for knowledge, pushing me deeper into the pages of the few books he had.

As April clouds left the hills, blossoms and wild flowers sprang up. The brown grass miraculously turned into deeper shades of green. Bees and birds were buzzing around us. The warmth of the Sun dispelled chills, and snow started to melt in the high hills and glaciers. Bhagirathi and Alaknanda were roaring down, and gradually I became familiar with every inch of the terrain.

In May, activity around Dev Prayag increased. Tourists and pilgrims came by the bus loads. Road repair teams were busy patching pot holes and landslides. At last the Badrinath temple doors were opened with fanfare and festivities. Roads closed during the winter months were now declared open and traffic escalated.

I noticed that Anand looked distracted and lost in thought. Also he was meeting other yogis from the area. He was discussing and planning something. When I asked him, he informed me that every year a group of sadhus travel on foot at this time of the year from Dev Prayag to Gangotri, and then to Badrinath, and back to Dev Prayag. This round trip usually last for about three months. In groups of five to ten, they climb over the Gomukh glacier, and travel through the Kalindi Pass, at a height of 19500 feet. The main purpose of this pilgrimage is to avoid the rush of tourists, and meditate in the tranquillity of the high alpine meadows. It is a privilege to be able to walk through the land of the Gods. There are no roads, just foot tracks, carved on the stones from thousands of years of bare feet travel by the yogis.

Finally the day came when Anand informed me that a few of them would start the journey early next morning. I had already expressed my desire to go with them, and was accepted. He advised me to carry two thick blankets.

"What about food?" I asked. "There are no shops there!"

"Don't worry about it," He laughed. "There are lots of berries and roots at this time of the year to satisfy your hunger. We don't kill any bird or animal, so if you hanker after non-vegetarian food, you will have to arrange for it yourself."

Next morning, before dawn we were on the road, choosing a mule track instead of the tarmac road.

"This track is much shorter, avoids human habitations and is less crowded. The route is beautiful, with wild flowers and walls of colourful foliage lining the path. We shall see wild animals and birds. Though this path is steep in places, we shall drink in the beauty and magnanimity of the mountains. On the whole it is much more preferable than the heavily congested road with diesel fumes and blaring horns, especially if you are on foot: less chance of being run over!"

There were five in the group including myself. I found it very difficult to judge their ages. Anand once told me that all of them were over sixty five years of age. We carried a small satchel containing toiletteries and a towel, a pen and a notebook. I also carried two thick blankets, one in my bag, and the other wrapped around my shoulders. We were similarly dressed, saffron garment around our waist in the traditional style of a 'Dhoti', and another draped over the shoulders. Our footwear consisted of wooden sandals. I had got accustomed to it.

"Yogis are impervious to weather changes." Anand had once told me in reply to my question. "We do not need warm clothes even in the sub-zero temperatures." I did not quite believe him then, thinking that he was pulling my leg. But now, when I found myself shivering despite wrapping a thick blanket, and the others seem not to feel the biting wind at all, I grudgingly and enviously believed him.

We were well amongst the wilderness by the time the Sun peered over the rim of the Eastern ranges. Wherever the golden light penetrated the foliage, dew drops sparkled and glittered, swayed and danced in unison with the wafting zephyr. Birds of various descriptions, from sparrows to woodpeckers, plain pigeons to the colourful paraquet twittered above us. We saw a few deer dart across our path, foxes slinking away and wild boars digging the earth with their snout, searching for root tubers. From time to time, when we skirted villages, cows and goats lifted their eyes to watch us go, most uncurious and utterly unconcerned. Sometimes small children would wave at us and follow us for short distances. We rested at intervals, picking ripe fruits and berries off the trees and shrubs along the path and quenching our thirst in rippling meandering mountain brooks. My companions spent a fair part of the day meditating, giving me time to observe nature as I had never done before. We were in no rush, and time was measured by the angle of the Sun, or absence of it. My stomach acted like a chronometer, warning me of the passage of time at regular intervals.

"Do you not fear wild animals?" I asked one evening. "We are not carrying any weapons to protect ourselves."

"Wild animals, especially predators fear us more than we fear them, and unless they are disabled with injury, old age or illness, they will avoid us." Anand replied and continued, "I once tried to tell you that this body was born to die, but nothing can harm your soul. In our journey through this world, our body act as a transport. It is our body that feels the emotions and the adversities, creating conflicts and illusions and fears in our minds. As yogis, it is our endeavour to detach ourselves from these illusions, and physical demands. If we succeed, only then can we hope for salvation."

I tried to rationalise what Anand said, but I could not accept his explanation. If we are to achieve salvation only when we discard all worldly desires, then why were we born, why do we live in this materialistic world? I kept my questions to myself for the moment, and mulled over them at night. The days were too pleasant and beautiful to dwell on serious or morbid thoughts.

A week's travel through idyllic natural trails brought us to Uttarkashi. We stayed at a dharmashala (cheap dormitory for pilgrims) for the night and visited the Krishna temple. My companions visited friends and acquaintances. I was new to the place and spent my time strolling through the bustling market place, with myriads of shops and impatient bus drivers blowing their horns to try and weave their vehicle through the congestion. The smell and sound seemed familiar, but I could not think when or where I had come across similar crowd and confusion. Everyone was busy, talking loudly to be heard through the cacophony of traffic noise. Uttarkashi is a small market town, the last on this leg of the road that ends at Gangotri, about one hundred kilometres from here. Regular bus and taxi service connects it to Hrishikesh, the nearest railhead, about one hundred and thirty kilometres and three to five hours away. Buses stop at many of the smaller towns and villages on the way.

On our way to Gangotri, we bathed in the hot water (sulphur) spring at Gauri-kund. The water from the actual sulphur spring is too hot and will scald. The water in mixed with cold water from a mountain spring, channelled and collected in a swimming pool size bath. This water is claimed to have medicinal properties.

We stayed the night in an 'Ashram' at Gangotri, where my companions met up with other yogis and 'sanyasis' who will also travel our route to Badrinath. Most of them knew each other. Some would travel with us, other would follow later. Since most of the year they spend in isolation in meditation, I suppose they take this opportunity to meet and update each other. Their conversation was dominated by the recent marine archaeological finds at Dwarka, on the Western coast of India, and other aspects of world religion that had raised controversies among scholars.

"Did you read about the underwater exploration at Dwarka?" Parashar asked Anand.

"Yes, the carbon dating of some of the artefacts appeared to indicate that the site is nearly ten thousand years old."

"Well at last we are getting physical confirmation of the factual nature of Mahabharata. The epic can no longer be ignored as mythology. The description of the last days of Dwarka is quite uncanny in view of the present find. According to Mahabharata, 'Arjun escorted the residents of Dwarka, numbering many millions. After all the people had set out, the ocean, the home of sharks, flooded Dwarka, which still teemed with wealth of every kind, with its waters. Whatever portion of ground was passed over by the departing citizens, ocean immediately flooded over with its waters.'

Another voice interrupted, "The general consensus is that the Rig Veda, the oldest of the Vedas, is more than ten thousand years old, but if the archaeologists can prove that Dwarka was submerged around ten thousand years ago, then that will push back the age of the Vedas even further in time. It must be exciting to the archaeologists involved in the dig."

Parashar took his cue, "I am sure, but it is a pity that marine archaeology is not very well developed in our country. They are dependent on sonar to map the sea bed, and under the silt. Dwarka was originally at the mouth of River Saraswati. Vedic settlements had flourished along the banks of River Saraswati, at one time the mightiest of the Indian rivers. It is assumed that it went underground (or dried up) around three thousand years ago. Satellite pictures do confirm the course of Saraswati. Civilization thrives on the banks of a flowing river and not a dried one, so it can be fairly assumed that the Vedic civilization was contemporary to the Harappan civilization, if not predating it."

Another voice piped in, "It is interesting to speculate. Just imagine the Pandavas may have been standing at this very place ten thousand years ago! How was it then? Was it more forested, more green or was it warmer? One thing is for sure, they did not get disturbed by honking of the buses and taxis."

The first voice added: "It amazes me how they travelled great distances. I know they had chariots, but surely chariot track was limited to only the main thoroughfares."

It was Parashar again, "What about using flying chariots? Ravan had one, and he lived many years before the Pandavas. If satellite pictures are to be believed, The Bridge that Ram built to reach Sri Lanka with his army from Rameshwaram and vanquished Ravan, was built many thousand years ago. Archaeologists have confirmed it to be man made. It again fits with mythology in geographical location and date. Imagine building a thirty kilometre long bridge built over ocean in antiquity that still stands nearly intact! Even the channel tunnel between UK and France is smaller than that. Some individuals could move very quickly through time and space. May be it was advanced technology, or just mind power. Certainly flying was not a common mode of transport, and as far as we know they had not invented the blasted horn."

"Archaeologists have a lot of work to do!" Anand commented with a smile.

"Do you know," Parashar was saying, "My hypothesis is that the Vedic culture had spread world wide, and the so called Pagans of Europe were also part of it. The word Pagan can easily be a distortion of the word Bhagwan (Bhagan → Pagan), the name Vedic people used for their Gods. I also believe we live through cycles of knowledge. The human race invents and discovers wonders and powers of nature, harnesses it and then becomes complacent. The evil in men rise, destroy all knowledge and semblance of civilization, taking us back to the dark ages, only to start developing again. Look around us today. Look at Iran, Afghanistan, the Talibans, Al-quaida, and most poignant of all—Baghdad: once a centre of culture and learning, now reeling from recent upheavals. During the medieval ages the Turks, the Mongols and the inquisition happy Catholic Church of that time did their best to suppress and destroy knowledge"

"Throughout history we find warlords and politicians destroying and desecrating centres of learning. Takshila University in western India was at its peak from about 800 BC to 800 AD. It had ten thousand

and five hundred students from all over the world, including Greece, China and Arabia. Sixty eight strains of knowledge were taught including medicine, surgery, economics, political science, warfare, astronomy and scriptures. Nalanda University in Eastern India was of equal eminence, with three thousand students. Students joined at the age of sixteen, after completing studies in their own country or region, and spent between four and eight years, mastering the subjects on offer, before retuning home, or taking up a post in the faculty. Eminent scholars like Bramagupta and Aryabhatta and Varahamihir had written treatise on the decimal system, algebraic principals, and the solar system with planets revolving around the Sun and held together by gravity, spherical nature of the Earth, and its rotation around its own axis etc. These were known and understood thousands of years before Copernicus and Newton had to re-discover the truth. Sushruta's method of rhinoplasty is used in modern day plastic surgery. Nearly two thousand five hundred years ago, he performed caesarean sections, operated on the brain, did cataract surgery etc. The Turks and Mongols who invaded and conquered the middle-east and then through the Khyber Pass came to India, destroyed and pillaged the land, burning all manuscripts, and executing people of knowledge. They feared knowledge—knowledge is power."

"The library of Alexandria was burnt. Even the Roman Empire, especially Emperor Constantine can be blamed for destroying many evidences of Pagan religion, and Christ's teachings that did not conform to the present day New Testament, including most of the apocrypha of apostles who were close to Christ, like Thomas and Mary, and knew from first hand experience more about Jesus. May be the Emperor needed everyone to believe in one Super human, Son of God in order to unite the fragmenting Roman Empire. May be that is why the early Roman Church could not allow a Jesus with a wife and children like other mortals, hence the vilification of Mary Magdalene.

After a short silence, the first voice said, "Teachings of Christ and Buddha are so similar in many ways, that some say Jesus was a Buddhist monk. Others say that later day Buddhist monks were influenced by Jesus. Since Buddha was born and reared in the Vedic tradition, and his teachings are not very different from Vedanta, there may be a third possibility, that both of them were singing from the same hymn book—The Upanishads.

Buddha had rebelled against the ceremonials, rituals, intrigues, insurrection and priest-craft of the Brahmins, and introduced a simple form of worship, and a religion of the heart based on the eternal truths or Upanishads. There are more than four hundred sects of present day Hinduism in India, based on Sanatan Dharma. The basic teaching remains the same, though each sect prefers to express their worship in different ways, Buddhism being one of them. The time when Buddha lived in India, and the turn of the first millennium AD, were both times of great disturbance and intrigue, insurrection, rebellions and wars. Such 'cusps in time' produce great men and great upheavals in the fabric of the society."

"Yes," Parashar interrupted, "In 249 BCE, Emperor Ashoka embraced Buddhism, and sent Buddhist monks to all parts of the known world, from Sri Lanka to Siberia, and Japan to Egypt. He made treatise with Greek kings, Antiochus of Syria, Ptolemaos of Egypt, Antigonus of Macedon, Magnus of Crene and Alexander of Epirus. These Buddhist monks lived among the people, and many of the local population adopted Buddhist practices, especially in the North Palestine region."

"Ancient Jews had three main sects, the Essenes, Pharisees and the Sadducees. The first two were liberal minded, and it is believed that the Gnostics who wrote the Nag Hamadi and Dead Sea Scrolls, belonged to the Essenes sect. They did not believe in rituals, and exalted individual personal transformation. They believed in seeking within for salvation. It is believed that John the Baptist and Jesus Christ belonged to this sect. Christ did not write any of his teachings, and many of the Gospels written by his apostles were burnt and destroyed, because the writings did not promote Emperor Constantine cause of uniting the Roman Empire. It is believed he killed his own son and wife on false suspicion, and massacred many who did not adhere to the teachings of the Church adopted in the Nocea council in 325AD."

"You are saying that all religions are basically similar, yet we seem to worship many Gods and Goddesses?" I asked.

"Sanatan Dharma is not idol worshipping. Idols help to focus your attention towards the Supreme Power and help towards self awareness. The rituals have the same purpose. A yogi, who is at a much higher level of spirituality does not need a temple or rituals or form to worship. Swami Vivekananda answering this question asked the questioner to spit on the portrait of his king. When the man hesitated, Swami asked him what the difference was between a piece of canvas and that portrait. For that matter, what is the difference between a piece of paper and a hundred dollar bill? It is our perception that matters, not the material. Many people worship a round piece of stone, yet it is not the stone that is being worshipped. The common man needs a finite object in front of him to focus his devotion. It is difficult for him to grasp the abstract Supreme Power called God. Once he learns to focus his mind, he can meditate without any prop for assistance."

"There are two aspects to Sanatan Dharma: 'Sruti' and 'Smriti'. The 'sruti' is the eternal truth, which does not change with time or geographical location. The Vedas and the Upanishad deal with this aspect of religion. 'Smriti' on the other hand changes with the prevalent practices of the society. Good habits and bad creep in as forms of rituals and traditions, which has nothing to do with religion in its pure form, but help groups to be motivated and focussed.

No religion is formed in isolation, and all cultures have borrowed from older civilisation. Sunday was holy day of the Pagans. Because Emperor Constantine wanted to distance himself from the Jews, he changed the Christian holy day from Sabbath to Sunday."

Anand stood up and stretched, "I think it is time to call it a day. Tomorrow we leave for Gomukh at dawn. In the final analysis, how does it matter who influenced whom or where civilisation evolved. As long as we keep faith, and follow the eternal truth, we should achieve salvation; we will gain knowledge and eternal bliss. The problem is that over the years barbarians have destroyed knowledge, and set the human race back whenever they seem to make some headway into answering the mysteries of nature."

We retired to our rooms. I lay awake for a long time, assimilating what I had heard that evening. Eventually I slept, a sleep interrupted with dreams of wars and strife and human suffering and hope. Anand shook me awake. The sky was still dark, with a few fading stars, a curved moon on the Western sky and a faint light beyond the Eastern hills. We went down to the river, and washed and bathed. The rustle of the fast flowing water in an otherwise silent dawn was pleasant, soothing and tranquil. Is it any wonder that holy men shun the human metropolis and towns to come here to meditate?

Gradually I saw others come down to the river. The sky became lighter, and purple and pink clouds appeared out of the darkness. Birds woke up and the peace of the early dawn was somewhat broken with stirring of life.

Our small group took to the mule track towards Gomukh, the glacier which gives rise to Bhagirathi, and eventually to the mighty Ganges. We will follow the river upstream to its source. The distance is only fourteen kilometres, but up and down over rock strewn tracks, intersecting brooks and negotiating hillocks. The track lay between ten and eleven thousand feet above sea level, and the vegetation reflected the altitude. Birch with yellow foliage and rhododendron bushes and orchids of various kinds lined the banks of the river. Early birds flitted in and out around us in search of worms, bold enough to come quite close to us. We walked in a single file, silently appreciating nature and lost in our own thoughts.

Until recently the glacier extended to Gangotri, hence the name: source of Ganges. Global warming has pushed the main glacier back, deeper into the folds of the Himalayas. Glacial activity is apparent at Gangotri, in the erosion of rocks, and the semicircular shallow waterfall. May be the rocks have a mixture of granite and limestone, because the semicircular rock formation, where the river takes a turn through ninety degrees and fall through fifteen feet, glitter white and orange, reminiscent of marble. Many 'rishis' (holy men) have their 'ashrams' at Gangotri, and stay there during the winter months, only to move up into the remoteness of the Himalayas in the summer to avoid bus loads of tourists, pilgrims and trekkers.

We followed the track hugging the left bank of Bhagirathi, towards its source. At times we were even up to a hundred feet above the bank, walking along the narrow ledge on an otherwise steep cliff, coming down in a gradual slope to the river. Across the river and ahead of us shoulders of serrated mountain rose up steeply to touch the clouds. The snow covered slopes mingling and disappearing into the white clouds. Sometimes the lone triangular white shape of the Shivaling peak showed up against a deep blue sky, behind the Bhagirathi peaks.

We saw very few wild animals, probably scared off by the press of the summer crowd. Most of us carried a staff to negotiate inclines. We did not have any watches or clocks, and judged time of day by the Sun. At hourly intervals we rested, sitting on flat rocks, and basking in the warmth of the morning Sun. The chill of the morning had dissipated with the emergence of and ascendance of the Sun.

We passed Chirwasa, the last tree line and the halfway mark to Gomukh. There was a large tea stall, and many tourists including small children, on their way back from Bhojwasa were having breakfast. Most of the tourists stay the night at Bhojwasa, four kilometres from Gomukh on their way back and make it to Gangotri the next morning. Although Gangotri has many hotels, Bhojwasa has only one rest house. We were in no hurry, and although all in our group looked fit and strong, they were elderly and did not believe in skipping from rock to rock or running down a slope. I must confess that I did do both, and at times would wait for them to catch up, gazing across at the mountains. At times sitting on a rock by the river, I would throw pebbles in the running water and see the ripples disappear in the current even before it had started to form. Often my eyes would follow the flight of eagles and kites, gliding near the clouds and over the hills. Occasionally a squirrel would scuttle across the path, probably scared off his feed by me. Except for the gurgling river, and rustle of the leaves announcing passage of gusts of wind through the foliage of birch and spruce and juniper, there was silence and peace and a sense of eternity. I was humbled just to imagine the millions of mornings these mountains and the river would have witnessed, the same Sunlight would have bathed them every morning. Are they bored standing there and watching the same view day after day, year after year, millennium after millennium? Are they curious to know who trudge the paths carved over their body, what song the birds sing, the language of thunder? Does the whisper of the wind still stir them out of their somnolence? I wondered.

We crossed Chirwasa, and the landscape became barren. Conifers and evergreens changed to scattered small shrubs perched next to bare rocks. The tree line presented a distinct change. The yellow leaves and white bark of the birch, green of the other conifers that I had grown so used to were conspicuous by their absence. We could see the Bhagirathi peaks covered with snow and the white triangular shape of the Shivalinga peak aloof in its majesty. We ambled at a leisurely pace. We were in no hurry, and reached Bhojwasa in the late afternoon. Most tourists do not travel beyond Gomukh, another four kilometres along the undulating track hugging the left bank of the Bhagirathi, returning back to Bhojwasa for the night. Others stay the night at Bhojwasa, preferring a longer return trip. Bhojwasa consist of a shallow valley with an alpine meadow, and a large rambling building sprawled over the meadow. The view though restricted, gives glimpses of the Himalayan splendour.

Most of our group travel this route every year, and know landmarks and wayside caves where they stop. They know where to find the fruits and the berries and roots to sustain nourishment. Their plan did not include scaling any peak. They wished to walk in the land of the Gods, and experience Divinity. The spirituality, serenity magnanimity and the breath-taking beauty of these mountains drag them year after year, facing the hardships and ardour of the journey. Gangotri is at a height of 10,000 feet above sea level, and our route will take us through Kalindi pass, at a height of 19,500 feet. One of the advantages of the slow progress is that the travellers get well acclimatised to the high altitude.

The innkeeper at Bhojwasa met us, and offered refreshments. A small dormitory was set aside for us. There were a lot of daylight hours left, and while the others sat to meditate next to Bhagirathi, I utilised the time exploring the surroundings. I stopped to drink some water from the river, and was surprised by the cold. It forcefully reminded me that this water was part of a glacier only four kilometres upstream. We had walked only about ten kilometres all day, and I was not tired. I walked up to the shoulder of the ridge forming the rim of a cup around the valley for a better view. My endeavour was amply rewarded. I sat on a rock and enjoyed the changing moods. As the

Sun slanted westward, and then dipped below the rim, flames shot across the sky, gradually getting dull, and eventually loosing its lustre and giving way to dusk. A thin mist had settled on the valley, and the evening star sparkled over the Shivalinga peak. The air felt cooler. I walked back to the inn, and sat on the steps with the others watching the end of the day. Shadows engulfed the valley, and the sky faded as darkness took hold. The peaks silhouetted against the sky lit only by the stars, waiting for the moon to rise above the rim. I shook out one of my blankets and wrapped it around my shoulders. I felt cold. The others seemed impervious to the sudden chill in the air, the certain drop in ambient temperature. This was the only time of the day when everyone sat together and discussed theology and philosophy or other relevant issues.

I woke up early next morning, and climbed to the vantage point I had discovered the day before, and waited for the day to come. The sky changed colours. The peak glistered gold, reflecting the rising Sun. Gradually the light filtered into the valley, and the ground mist cleared. I walked down to the river. I could see the sandy bottom through crystal clear water. The white rapids breaking on the submerged stones rustled past. I kneeled on the bank and washed my face. I found the river too cold to enter, and decided to defer taking a bath and wait for the Sun to be well up in the sky. My stomach was growling, and I walked back in search of breakfast. Most of our group were waist deep in the river, facing the Sun, which was still hidden behind the hills, and praying. I found myself alone with the innkeeper. He offered me a hot cup of tea and 'puri-sabji.' He was curious to see me in this group. I recounted my experience to him and tried to satisfy his curiosity. We were talking at length about the tourist trade, the weather, and other innocuous subjects, when Anand, Parashar and a few others walked in. The innkeeper shifted his attention, and greeted them, and set about attending to their needs. I was quite full and was contented to sit back and watch the hustle and bustle of activity around me.

We took to the tracks early, and by the time the Sun peeped over the Eastern peaks into the valley, we had reached Gomukh. The Sunlight reflected off the glacier giving iridescence, reflected in the water at its foot. The glacier was about forty feet high, a bluish green stratified cliff of ice with a shallow overhang, where the warm Earth has scalloped chunks of ice from it. Streams were flowing in from a wide frontage of the glacier, running in rivulets and joining up at a distance. The pebble strewn bed between the shallow rivulets was easy to cross. In fact anyone wishing to access the right bank of Bhagirathi, and climb peaks like the Shivaling or the Meru, have to cross Bhagirathi at this point, and retrace their way along the right bank towards Gangotri for a few kilometres to the reach the break in the rocks and the glacier, giving access to those mountains.

We rested for a while, drank the cold water and then continued on our way. The track wound around the base of the glacier, and carved its way along a slope, to reach the top. It was a land very different from the one below. Blocks of ice rather than stones formed the relief around us. Lichens and short shrubs had grown in the cracks. WE crossed the glacier and reached Tapovan, literally meaning a garden for meditation: a thin strip of grassy meadow along a frozen stream, surrounded by steep hills and large rocks at a height of 14870 ft. A trickle of water ran down, and we followed it to reach the cave. The cave had a narrow opening but widened out to a large hall inside, the roof sloping up forming a high ceiling. Sometime in the past, passage of water must have hollowed out the cave, which for thousand of years had been used by Rishis and pilgrims as temporary shelter. Outside, some wild berries grew along the stream, flanked by orchids and wild flowers.

I ate a handful of berries, drank the cold water of the stream, sat down on a rock with my back to the warm Sun and facing the high white triangles against the azure sky and flitting cirrus clouds. We were fourteen thousand feet above sea level. The air was thin. I was feeling out of breath after the short climb. I let the warmth seep through my body, closed my eyes and let my mind wander. I moved back in time to 1500 BCE. In my mind's eye I saw a few sages sitting in the lotus position in the valley next to the stream, deep in meditation. Near the cave a young Brahmin woman sat with a boy of twelve. The woman was dressed in a simple unstitched home-spun cotton fabric like a saree, and her long black hair was piled high over her head in a coiffure. The boy was reciting verses from the Vedas. Whenever he made a mistake, or hesitated for the right word, the smiling woman corrected her son, and encouraged him.

The Vedas, literally meaning knowledge, were compiled by ancient philosophers and seers and scientists and yogis thousands of years ago, over many years. There were many women who contributed; they were as literate, intelligent and perceptive as the men, and discoursed on philosophical and scientific matters on equal terms with the men in those days. The Vedas contain knowledge on all aspects of life: spirituality, medicine, surgery, economics, commerce, music, politics, warfare etc. Women in ancient India had a strong voice in all aspects of their society.

At the end of the first millennium, though the society was at its zenith in learning, culture and riches, decadence had set in. The rich and the powerful became lazy and greedy; too busy pandering to their pleasures to notice the weakness in the society. Religious dogmas and bad practices became rife. Caste system that was originally created to ease civic administration, took the ugly form of untouchability. Caste system in its fundamental form exist in all countries and societies: All have teachers, administrators, businessmen or entrepreneurs and the unskilled workers. In India, around that time, caste system, which was hereditary, became very rigid and the lower castes were shunned by the upper classes, depriving them of any social advancement, irrespective of merit. The society started to break up. A thousand years of foreign occupation followed. There was looting in grand scales, desecration and destruction of temples, and dismantling of ancient heritage and culture, leaving India a poor illiterate country, lacking in self esteem, pride and self confidence, forced to beg for foreign aid, and looked down by the rest of the world. Thousands of temples were destroyed, Mohammed of Gazni raided just one temple in Gujrat, the Somnath temple seventeen times, each time carrying away caravans loaded with jewels and ornaments, killing million, enslaving others who were sold later in Arabia and Africa. Mohammed Khilji, Qutubuddin, and the Moghals, with the exception of Akbar, continued in the same tradition, forcefully converting the local population to Islam. Most of the Jesuits came with the East India Company, went to the remote villages to teach and preach and spread the word of Christ. The tribals and the untouchables who were ostracised, made social outcasts, and often starved due to poverty, welcomed them, converting to the new religion. It is a miracle that the Vedic culture still exists. It has paid a heavy price for the selfish few who dared to demean humanity. The land of gold had turned into one of the poorest countries in the world.

I had fallen asleep. The setting Sun had stirred a cool breeze that woke me up. I saw people were collecting firewood, and I joined them. We gathered a big pile of dry twigs in the cave. We lighted a small fire. Darkness cloaked the valley, lighted only by a sliver of Moon and a few bright stars. Some of us gathered around the fire, while others were either in deep meditation or watching the approaching night. There was peace and quiet. Not many insects or birds live at this altitude. The usual night sounds were thus muted.

"The other day while discussing religion, someone mentioned that God is present in every living and non living object around us, and that we must live in harmony with nature. Could you please explain and elaborate on it?" I asked Anand.

"Do you know the legend of Vishnu's fourth incarnation?" Anand asked me. "King Hiranyakashapu was vain and cruel king, proud of his strength. He believed himself to be more powerful than God, and when Pralhad told him that God is everywhere, he pointed to a stone pillar in the foyer of his palace, and asked if God was present in it. When Pralhad said yes, the king became very angry and kicked the pillar. A strange creature, half human and half lion emerged from the pillar and killed the king."

"We believe in God's existence in every animate and inanimate object in this universe. God is not a person, but a power, an energy that pervades this universe. We worship Him in various forms. The form we choose is for our own convenience to understand something that is beyond comprehension. For thousands of years our sages have told us that we are all part of the great power we call God. Quantum physics has given us logical proof of this phenomenon we had for so long accepted in good faith."

"In 1935 Albert Einstein, Nathan Rosan and Boris Podosky proposed through flawless mathematical reasoning that if the quantum theory were correct, then 'A change in the spin of one particle in a two particle system would affect its twin simultaneously, even if the two have been widely separated in the mean time.' This concept ran contrary to Einstein's Special Theory of Relativity that forbids the supposition of transmission of any signal (energy) faster than the speed of light. Obviously a signal telling the particle 'What to do' have to travel faster than light if instantaneous change were to occur between the particles. This dilemma came to be known as the ERP effect. In 1964 Bell's Theorem seemed to uphold the ERP effect, and in 1972, Clauser confirmed the statistical predictions of quantum mechanics, working with an elaborate system involving photons, calcites crystals and photo multiplier tubes. The experiment has since been run several times with the same consistent result. The signal controlling the particles has to be something other than energy. We call it consciousness. I suppose this forms the basis for telepathy."

"One of the implications of this phenomenon is that everything in this universe is part of a whole, and that whole is God. Like a hologram, every part of the whole has the capacity to project the whole. When we get to the state of God consciousness, or salvation, we become God like, we merge with God. Many holy men from different religions have attained this state. They could harness the power of nature, perform miracles."

"Consider genetics for example. We know that the whole human structure with individualised traits and characteristics are encoded in the chromosomes in each cell. Potentially each cell can replicate the whole man. This phenomenon is called cloning. There are many genes in the chromosomes that appear to have no function. Is it possible that they are coded to represent the universe around us? The concept is that everything in this universe is part of a whole, and that the whole is represented in every part of it, animate or inanimate—somewhat like the hologram."

"There are no individuals in the cosmos. What is it that we call an individual? Is it the body or the power and energy that drive it! The body will perish, but the energy, the engine of life will be recycled to drive another body. In our philosophy self has no meaning, individuality is an illusion. You came into this world naked, devoid of any possessions, and you will leave in the same state. You cannot take any wealth or property with you. Social status, achievements, richness, family ties—these are all illusions, put in our path to distract us from seeking the eternal truth."

"During Dassehra, the ten day festival to commemorate the victory of Divine Power (Durga) in a feminine form over evil is worshipped, clay idols are constructed. Until the clay idols are placed on a pedestal on the sixth day, the idol is not considered to be a deity, but a mannequin. Again when worship is over, on the tenth day the idol is immersed in water, where the clay melts and merges with the silt of the river bed. We do not worship the idol, we worship what it represents, the Divine Power, the abstract that is very difficult to quantify, visualise or understand for the common man."

"Supreme state of God consciousness is that state of knowledge and realisation where all dualities vanish, where all ideas of separateness cease forever, and where tremendous on rush of the Divine essence of Universal Spirit, breaking down all barriers and limitations of our human consciousness causes us to realise our eternal oneness with the Heavenly Father on the spiritual plane."

"We acknowledge the usefulness of our body to conduct physical activities, to procreate, perform social and moral duties and obligations: In doing so we learn about the Divine Power, the eternal truth. When the body withers, the power within discards it. The body, made of the five elements will break down into its component parts. If anyone tries to preserve it, it stinks and rots. If mummified, it looks grotesque and inhuman. The body has finished its usefulness when the power leaves it. That is why we burn dead bodies."

We stayed in Tapovan for a few days. The weather was usually bright and crisp, warm during the day and cold at nights. The afternoons in mountains are very unpredictable. Invariably there would be clouds, covering the Sun, and showers are not uncommon. By nightfall, the sky would clear up again. We moved on, not very far, only another six kilometres, keeping to similar altitude to reach Nandanvan, another alpine meadow. This place is much wider, and is in the bowl at the foot of the Bhagirathi peaks. As in Tapovan, a convenient cave was found, and I spent a time of idyllic inactivity except for collecting firewood and berries. While the others meditated, I explored the surroundings. I was surprised to see the streams teeming with trout. Obviously no one has ever fished in these waters.

After a week's sojourn at Nandanvan, we picked ourselves to climb up to Vasuki Tal, a glacial lake at 16000 ft, trekking along the Chaturangi glacier. Blocks of ice floated in the crystal clear sweet water of the lake. The reflections of the snow covered peaks in the shimmering blue water was an unforgettable sight. We stayed by the lake for a week. Weather Gods were kind to us, and granted us blue skies, bright Sunshine and a star filled night sky. It was nearing New Moon, and the stars looked bigger and brighter.

We skirted the Sweta glacier, and crossed Khara Pathar, consisting mainly of moraine. We spent a couple of nights in a cave there. We had been steadily climbing, and the air was growing thinner. Our next stop took us beyond the Sweta glacier, to Kalindi base. Through breaks in the mountain ranges to the South of us we could see rolling hills of diminishing heights going down to the horizon, perhaps to meet the plains. We skirted a few deep gorges. We could see the foaming white water rapids. Despite the height, we could hear the roar of the current. We stayed a few nights at the Kalindi base. It was a picturesque place.

We woke up before Sunrise on a clear morning, and took to the final climb of our track. We had a long way to go, more than twelve kilometres to get over the Kalindi Pass at a height of 19500, and down the other side to a suitable camp site. Though we were well acclimatised, and were walking slowly, I was getting out of breath, needing to stop frequently. No one was complaining for the view was breath taking and beyond description. With reluctance we started our descent, reaching Raj Parav by evening. We were all tired that night, and I went to bed early, waking up with the first light.

We were nearing the end of our pilgrimage, and I felt depressed, knowing that very soon I shall have to make a decision as to where I want to go, what I wish to do. We descended gradually to Arwatal and then to Gastoli and Mana. I was pleased to be below the tree line, and in the familiar, lightly forested land of deep gorges and fast rivers. The birds and animals I had been missing in the higher altitudes were all here. There were people we would meet from time to time, villagers out in the forest cutting firewood or collecting honey. The impish, surprised faces of children staring at us, in the middle of their game, temporarily suspended, interrupted by the passage of strangers. We bathed in the hot water lake at Badrinath and visited the Vishnu temple. At Badrinath I had a sense of déja-vu. I felt that I had been there before. The previous visit appeared to have great significance, and I also felt a sense of great loss. I could not understand my feelings. I spoke to Anand about it, and he advised me to be patient. We prayed at the temple. We stayed at Badrinath for a few nights, and then it was time to disperse. Autumn was setting in; the night air was getting chilly. It was September. The Badrinath temple doors would be closed at the end of the month, and traffic would cease. The roads beyond Joshimath would be snowed under. It had been almost a year since Anand rescued me from the River.

THE BUSINESSMAN

I stared at the reflection of the setting Sun. pilgrims bathing on the steps of Har-ki-pauri were silhouetted against the red glow. The waves lapped over the stone steps, cleaning all muddy footprints left by hawkers and pilgrims and beggars. There was coolness in the air after a hot day. I could hear the traffic noise. A few street lights were switched on in anticipation of the oncoming envelope of darkness. Peels of brass bells resonated, drowning the cacophony of homeward bound tired birds.

I felt my elation slowly ebb away and settle down to a sense of deep satisfaction. I felt at peace with the world around me. Today I got the results of my degree examination, and I passed with honours in economics. Now I am a graduate. I have spent the last four years at Hardwar. Four years of hard work and hand to mouth living. An existence bound by routine, the only escape was when exhaustion rolled a blanket of sleep over me. I woke up early and slept late. I was always desperately short of time to fit in my activities. I had worked during the day to earn a living and studied at night. Four years of frequenting the local public library. I was feeling nostalgic and remembering my days with Anand. He would have been happy for me. Today I did not have anyone to share my happiness with. I was alone.

I had left Anand at Dev Prayag in October that year and came down to Hardwar. Anand had given me a contact address. His friend Vinod Verma ran a hotel and a restaurant for tourists and pilgrims. Vinod was in his early sixties, short and plump with a bald head and a beaming clean shaven face. He was energetic and always on the move. He directed me to a youth hostel, and employed me as the night manager in his hotel. He advised me to get around in town and learn about all the important places and customs. As a tourist guide to supplement my income from his hotel, he thought I could earn enough to live comfortably.

I enrolled at the local night school and then the university. The classes were held in the evenings, before I started my shift work at the hotel as the night manager. Nights were usually quiet, and I managed a few hours sleep. During the day I escorted tourists and pilgrims, visiting the various temples and the river bank. Many religious rites are performed on the banks of River Ganges. Many pilgrims came to Hardwar only to take a dip in the holy river.

Very soon I had settled down into a routine. I would contact my clients and show them around, helping them to visit the temples and keeping them away from touts and conmen. They paid me a fixed rate for my services. I would attend classes in the evenings and go back to the hotel by ten every night to start my shift there. My expenses were negligible and very soon I saved up a comfortable nest egg.

As a guide I came in contact with a cross-section of men and women from various walks of our society. Some came for pilgrimage, to please the Gods, some were just curious about the place. Others came as tourists to experience the sights and sounds of the sub-Himalayan Tarai region. Most came by cars or buses, availing modern conveniences. Only a few determined pilgrims walked long distances to reach Har-ki-pauri, as Hardwar is also known, believing that the hardship will assure blessings of the Gods. They came from all over

India and beyond. Their faith drew them to the holy shrines and to the 'Ghats' (paved river banks, with steps leading into the water) of Har-ki-pauri.

Religion is big business all over the world, and this town is no exception. The fear of the supernatural, the greed for wealth and success and attempts to make the path to the after life smoother are some of the reasons people pay enormous sums of money, hoping to bribe God. The God-men and the conmen reap a bonanza. Astute businessmen, highly acclaimed academics, politicians and people from the show biz all empty their purse at the feet of the Gods. I had a nice steady income. Over the years I had saved up enough to start a new venture. I became restless and wanted to break away from this monotonous meaningless existence. I realised that the time has come for me to move on.

A few faces flitted through my thoughts. Mr Suresh Sharma had come with his family to get Lord Shiva's blessings in order to expand his business. His eldest daughter was just married and the newly weds had also come to escape the blistering heat of New Delhi. Mr Sharma owned a successful local newspaper, and wished to turn it into a national daily. He had contacted many other regional paper owners and enlisted their help, often buying into their business, especially in the major cities and towns. He believed that everyone and everything can be bought for the right price, including Gods and God-men. Unfortunately for him the thieves and the pickpockets had marked him for plucking.

Thus one morning the family found themselves with no money or jewellery. They had been cleaned out at night as they slept. Even their expensive jackets and coats were missing. Never having encountered a situation where he did not have the upper hand, he fumed and fretted. He blamed the hotel management, and went to the police station. He tried to bluster his way in, intimidating the constables.

Unfortunately he rubbed the senior police officer the wrong way when he tried to undermine his authority by trying to call up the regional police commissioner. He got a rude shock when he was told to file his complaint and leave the police station, and stop interfering with police work. He tried to throw his weight around, but since no one knew him, no one paid much attention to him. He had never been in a situation in his life where he was of no account, and he was not pleased with the experience.

He tried to ring up his desk editor and his bank manager but due to fault in the telephone line, he could not contact them. He found himself cut off from all contacts. He did not believe in plastic cards, and was not carrying any credit card. He realised at long last that without money he could not even buy lunch or pay for his hotel room. That realisation shook him. He felt helpless. I offered to loan him some money, enough to pay for his hotel bill, lunch and taxi fare to New Delhi. He was a proud man and did not want to take loan from a lowly tourist guide. He had no choice however, and mumbled thanks when I handed him the money. I could see that it hurt his pride to be in a position where he had to beg money for food. With reluctance he accepted money from me. He returned the money with a thank you note within a week. I wondered if he would remember me after more than two years.

Mr Banik was a moneylender in Delhi. He was not a very religious man, but his mother insisted on visiting Har-ki-pauri before her death and forced him to accompany her. He was relieved when he realised that he can safely leave his mother in my care, and did not have to trawl through all the temples. His mother was quite happy when she left, and that pleased Mr Banik. He left me his card and asked me to look him up if and when I went to Delhi.

Nikhil Gupta was a successful lawyer, practising in Delhi High Court. He headed a well known law firm, and had good political connections.

While bathing at the Ghat, his youngest daughter, aged twelve years lost her footing, and was swept away by the current. Somehow I managed to pull her out of the water and the grateful Guptas invited me to visit them, and to let them know if I needed help of any kind. They would be happy to oblige if it was within their power. Mrs Gupta was especially tearful and pleaded that I must visit them if ever I went to Delhi.

Strangers came to stay at our hotel, and it had been a hobby of Mr Verma's, the hotel owner and our employer, to try and predict the actual profession of men and women registered, or whether the couple were actually married. Most often the speculations remained unconfirmed, but once in a while we were exposed to human foibles. Whenever Mr Verma's speculations were proven to be correct, he derived immense satisfaction. These aspects of the human character would have remained hidden from me had I not been directly involved in some of the cases as the hotel manager.

One day a middle aged man checked in with his pretty young wife. I gathered they were planning to visit the 'Valley of Flowers' after a few days at Hardwar and Hrishikesh. They did not appear very religious, or interested in visiting the local attractions. They spent most of their time in the room, and ordered meals through room-service. He claimed to be a lawyer from Chandigarh, and appeared to have a lot of money. He was quite free with his tips to the hotel staff. I assumed they were newly married on their honeymoon, but Mr Verma was a cynical man, and was positive that they were love-birds on an adulterous relationship away from their circle of acquaintances.

Mr Verma's suspicions proved to be correct. A week after they had left, a lady in her mid forties came to our hotel, looking for a middle aged man that fitted our departed lawyer's description. She claimed that she was looking for her husband. Her husband was a sales representative in a pharmaceutical company, and his job involved touring his area of responsibility. He had informed his wife that he would be going to Agra for a few days. She became suspicious when one of her friends claimed to have seen him at the railway station boarding a train to Hrishikesh, accompanied by a pretty young lady. Hrishikesh was in the opposite direction to Agra from their hometown. Her mind went back to the day of his departure, when she had seen him packing expensive aftershave and cologne in his travel bag, quite out of character for him. At the time she wanted to quiz him, but thought better of it in order not to embarrass him. She also found that he had made a large withdrawal from their joint account before leaving. Not having heard from her husband for a week, she decided to investigate.

Mr Verma, though pleased to have his suspicion confirmed, was reluctant to get involved in a messy divorce law-suit. He declined all knowledge of the man. When I asked him why he lied, he defended his action by claiming to protect the wife from emotional trauma.

One night I received a frantic call from a first floor room. The lady shrieked into the telephone that her husband was in server pain, and could not breathe. I rang a local doctor with whom we had an arrangement for emergency cover. I also rang the local taxi agency in case we needed to transfer the gentleman. I went upstairs and found an elderly gentleman bathed in sweat and gasping for breath. His lips were blue and he looked pale. Though it was late November and there was a chill in the air, I opened the windows and tried to prop him up in the bed with pillows. The doctor came within the next fifteen minutes, and thought the man was suffering from a heart attack. He gave him some morphine injection and we bundled him and his wife into the waiting taxi for transfer to the local district hospital. Surprisingly, he survived. After a week in hospital he was discharged.

I discussed the matter with Mr Verma and asked him if we could keep oxygen cylinders and a stretcher in the hotel for such emergencies. He agreed to think over it, since such situations are rare, and keeping oxygen cylinders can be hazardous. He agreed to buy a folding stretcher to facilitate carrying unwell people down the stairs. It was a cheaper option than to installing lifts.

In a way being the night manager of a hotel helped me to get customers. Quite often I was asked by new arrivals to help them get around, and offering my services as their guide for a fee was the logical next step.

I did have my share of excitement and encountered situations I was not equipped to deal with. A young couple booked into our hotel for three nights. They planned to travel on to Badrinath. The lady was heavily pregnant, and I had my doubts about the wisdom of such a plan. However as events unfolded, my fears were justified. I found myself in a situation testing my fortitude, patience and resourcefulness.

On the second night, around ten O'clock the man asked me for a bottle of hot water, saying that his wife was having cramps in her tummy. A couple of hours later he came down saying that the pains were getting worse, and could I ring for a doctor. Not having dealt with pregnant women in the past, it never occurred to me that the lady may be going into labour. I rang one of our local doctors. He came and gave me an earful for not telling him that the lady in question was in late stage of pregnancy and that she was in labour. He asked me to arrange with a private maternity home for her admission, and to shift her there. When I discussed the matter with the husband, I realised that he was not carrying enough money to afford private care, especially if she were to have a complicated delivery. I found myself out of my depth, and called Mr Verma at his residence. He sounded very grumpy over the telephone at being woken up in the middle of the night.

"Is this her first child?" he asked, and I relayed the question to the father to be.

"Yes," He replied.

"Well, there is no need to panic. You have plenty of time. Book a taxi to come around at six in the morning, and take her to the municipal maternity home." He replaced the receiver.

I did as advised, and sent the husband upstairs with more hot water for the water-bottle. I had dozed off when frantic shouts of the man and shaking of my shoulders woke me up. I rubbed sleep out of my eyes, and tried to calm him down. I gathered from his garbled speech that the lady had passed a lot of water and some blood, and she thought that delivery of the baby was imminent. I was fully awake and alert by now, and grabbed the phone to bark at the taxi night desk for a large taxi urgently. We ran upstairs, and found her writhing with spasmodic pain. Never having seen such a sight, I felt very scared.

"Can you take her downstairs?" I asked the man, and immediately realised the foolishness of the question. She was in no position to walk down the stairs, and he was not strong enough to carry her. Without another word, I scooped her in my arms when she appeared a bit settled and not thrashing about, and went down the stairs. The taxi had arrived, and asking the driver to open the rear door, I laid her in the back seat. The husband jumped into the front seat, and off they went at top speed through the empty streets of pre-dawn, still sleeping town of Hardwar, and I heaved a sigh of relief.

I learnt a valuable lesson, never to assume the obvious. Working in the hotel was an eye opener, and a good grooming ground for developing a devious mind. Looking back over the years and the various encounters with people, I realised that I had a wealth of contacts whose hearts I had touched at their moments of weakness and vulnerability. They listened to me, and accepted me as their friend or well wisher when they were away from their habitat, and were apprehensive of the unknown. I wondered whether these men and women would remember me now that they are back in their comfort zone, cocooned in a sheltered society where they pull the strings. I had kept a diary with their contact details. I did not intend to call on them unless I had to. I wanted to meet them as their equal, and not someone begging their indulgence.

I knew the time had come for me to make a move, but I was not sure where to go or what to do. After talking to visitors and my acquaintances, I came to the conclusion that Delhi was the place to be. The capital city offered many opportunities. I decided to leave and bade farewell to my friends and colleagues.

Change is never easy. Human mind has an inherent desire to cling to the past, and fears change; the unknown. I suppose it is the inertia to change that allows communities to be built, and permanency in society to be developed, interdependence and social interactions to flourish. Yet without change bad practices and greed creep in, petty squabbles fester and erupt into riots and social disturbances. Human values are lost leading to destruction of civilizations. From time to time men and women with pioneering spirit stride out looking for a new world and make our world a better place.

I stood on the railway platform in Delhi and looked around. Crowd was rushing around me, pushing and dodging, swearing and gesticulating. Everyone seemed to be in a hurry. Porters carrying heavy cases on their turbaned heads jostled me. I realised standing and watching was not a safe option. I joined the move towards the exit. I was not carrying much luggage. I handed my ticket to the checker and stepped into the bright sunshine of the late morning.

I was near an auto rickshaw stand, and looked around uncertainly. A young driver nearer my age pulled up his auto rickshaw in front of me and asked if I wished to go anywhere. I gave him an address, not very far from the railway station and asked him how much he would charge me. I was expecting him to ask for an exorbitant amount, and take me for a ride. He surprised me by telling me that the address was only a kilometre away and since I was not carrying much luggage, I could walk the distance if I so desired.

"I am new to Delhi," I said. "Why don't you take me there? I'll pay you by the meter."

"Get in." He said.

The night before leaving Hardwar, Mr Verma had invited me to dinner at his place. His wife had prepared a gourmet spread. Though I indulged myself, and ate with abandon, I could not do justice to the feast laid out in front of me. I had to apologise for having no more appetite. Mr Verma then took me to his study and started asking me my plans. I was quite frank with him, and told him that I did not have any set plan. Everything was nebulous, and would depend on the time and place. He was not satisfied with my answer.

"You must never make a move without knowing your mind." He said. "I have a friend who owns a hotel like mine in Paharganj, near New Delhi railway station. I know he is looking for a night manager, and since you are experienced at such a job, I can recommend you to him. Stay there for a few months and learn the city. Try to understand the dynamics and the economics of the local population. Find out the people who make the businesses move and rake in all the profits. Try and develop a network of informers. Always try to know about things before they happen. In business knowledge is money. Once you think you have found your feet, establish a base and go to work. Do not ignore anyone, even the poorest man and do not be overawed by the wheelers and dealers of the society. Just remember that we are all mortals and have our shortcomings. We all must die one day. If ever you feel like packing up, you can come back to Hardwar. I'll always be happy to employ you in my business."

"You are in an enviable position," Mr Verma continued. "You have no dependents, no ties, no one to hold you back. You can achieve whatever you want; your only limiting factor will be your imagination or lack of it, your appetite for success and your ambition."

I thanked his wife and him for a lovely evening and left. I experienced a warm glow of kinship. It felt good to know that I can fall back if my venture fails. At times such thoughts can be a disadvantage though, and may tempt me to give up more easily when faced with difficulties.

Shamim, the auto rickshaw driver lived in one of the pokey flats near LNJP hospital on the other side of the railway station. He supported a younger brother and a sister. Both his parents were invalid, suffering from tuberculosis.

"Here you are," he said stopping the vehicle in front of a three storey building in a less crowded broad road with shady trees lining the pavements. A board above the main door, proclaimed the building to be "Ashoka Hotel". The building was attractive with yellow eaves and light blue window shutters. The main door opened on to the pavement, and there was no porch.

I paid Shamim and said, "Come and meet me whenever you are passing this way. I don't know anyone in the city and could do with some friends." He smiled, waved his hand, whipped the auto rickshaw around and was gone, the engine screaming protest at the acceleration, leaving behind exhaust fumes: the noise fading rapidly as he disappeared in the distance round a corner. I watched him as far as I could and then transferred my attention to the building that was to be my home for some months, I hoped. Most of the buildings on this road were business premises; all had boards declaring their purpose. This obviously was not a residential area.

I picked up my suitcase and walked into the hotel. The receptionist was busy with a customer. I waited. The foyer was small but tastefully decorated in Rajasthani style—colourful and complete with two elephants next to the door. There was a three-seat sofa against the far wall. I took a seat, keeping my suitcase close to me. The interior was invitingly cool and a bit dark. Heavy curtains shielded the room from the midday glare of the Sun. A pedestal fan was oscillating its head, stirring up a breeze that cut through the sultry atmosphere.

The receptionist, a pleasant young girl in her early twenties, was free at last and looked at me. I walked up to her and asked if I could see Mr Kartar Singh. She enquired my business, and I handed her the introductory letter Mr Verma had given me for Mr Singh. She excused herself, and went inside the hotel, asking me to take a seat. She came back presently, followed by a tall well built middle aged Sikh gentleman. He wore a blue turban and his flowing black beard peppered with white was curbed with tight netting draped across his chin from ear to ear. This netting is a dress accessory commonly used by that community. He was comfortably attired in a white 'salwar' and 'kurta'. A steel bangle was shining through the cuff on his left wrist. He wore gold rimmed spectacles, and overall presented an impressive figure.

I stood up as they approached me, and I joined my hands together in the traditional style of salutation and said, "Namaste. I am Amar. Mr Vinod Verma asked me to meet you. I was working in his hotel until recently."

"Yes. He has given you a glowing reference. Welcome to Delhi." He turned to the young lady and introduced her, "This is my younger daughter Sunita. She manages the daily operations. I have other businesses as well." He paused for a moment, and then added, "I am happy for you to work here as the night manager. I don't think this job will be any different to what you were doing at Hardwar. Sunita will look after you. I'll see you later in the evening." He nodded at us, and left to finish whatever he was doing when Sunita interrupted him.

Sunita smiled at me when we were left alone. She had an attractive smile. At five feet seven inches, she was not much shorter than me. Her lithe figure and graceful movements were a pleasure to watch. She had large dark eyes in an oval face, and wisps of curly hair escaped her ribbons and played over her face, being blown by the fan. An impatient hand would admonish it from time to time as it tickled her cheek or got into her eyes. She was fairer than average sikh girls, her cheeks crimson from the afternoon heat. Her generous mouth framed by red lips was speaking to me: "Have you had lunch? Or are you hungry! If you are, don't hesitate to say so. I think I can offer you lunch." When I declined her offer, she said, "I'll take you upstairs to a single room. You can live there until you find alternative accommodation." I followed her carrying my suitcase, and was shown to a small room with a single bed. "You have to share the toilet and the shower room I am afraid," she said. "This room is not en-suite."

"I have no problem with this room," I assured her.

"Well, in that case I'll leave you to settle down. If you need anything see me downstairs. I assume you will like to start working tomorrow. We'll talk more about it later when you come down." She flashed another smile at me, and left.

One thing I noticed as I was climbing the stairs was that there was no lift in this hotel. My nocturnal experiences at Hardwar flitted through my mind, and I decided that I needed to discuss contingency plans for evacuation of people from the upper floors with Sunita and Mr Kartar Singh.

Though the room was small, it was pleasant. A large window overlooked the tree tops shielding the road in front of the hotel. The room was airy. A ceiling fan running at full speed kept it cool. The bed was pushed against a wall away from the window, and had fresh linen on the mattress. A writing table and a comfortable chair occupied the other wall. I was feeling tired from the unaccustomed heat and the travel. I pulled the curtains shut to darken the room, changed into pyjamas, and hit the bed.

I woke up a few of hours later, much refreshed. The day was far gone, and as I threw the curtains open, the late afternoon Sun streamed into my room. I made a trip to the toilet and washed my face. Changing into fresh clothes, I walked down to find Sunita still sitting hunched over a computer at the reception. There was another girl of Sunita's age at the reception. She looked up as I entered. As I walked up to the reception Sunita looked up and smiled at me. She pointed to the other girl and said, "This is Radha. She works as a receptionist during the afternoon and early evening." Then she turned to face Radha and introduced me: "And this is Amar, who is going to be the night manager."

We said hello to each other and I asked Sunita if she wanted me to hang around. She was busy, and asked me to finish whatever I had in mind. She would talk to me later. I waved at them and walked out of the hotel. I wanted to familiarise myself with the neighbourhood and took to the streets. I was back in a couple of hours, and found Shamim waiting for me.

"Have you been waiting long?" I asked.

"No. I have just come, and was going to ask for you," Shamim said.

I introduced him to Sunita and Radha, and then took him to the other corner initially, and sat on the sofa but as the foyer was getting crowded with new arrivals trying to check in, we went to my room.

"I came to see how you are getting on," Shmaim commented on the way. "I was passing this way after dropping a customer at another hotel in your row.

"I have been offered a job, and going to start tomorrow evening. I'll be working the nights."

Shamim was a graduate from Delhi University. He did not have any honours. After trying for jobs in government services and banks for a year, he decided to run the auto rickshaw (taxi) service. His home condition was not very good. His father was a retired railway employee on a meagre pension. Fortunately he did not have to buy medicines, which was paid for by the railways. Practically he was the sole earner. After having no luck in the job market, he took the bold step of taking a bank loan to start his business. He bought the auto rickshaw, drove it during the day, and rented it out to a friend of his for the night. He had been doing this for the past three years. The auto rickshaw is getting old, and he will have to change it soon. He had managed to save some money and pay off the bank loan.

Shamim's father had bought the flat from Delhi Development Authority ten years ago, and is now in a poor state of repair, with the roof leaking and the walls needing a lick of paint. Still it was home, a place to live. Cities are quite expensive places to live, and very impersonal. They don't care if you live or die. It is always a struggle to make ends meet. On the whole he was coping fairly well with his business and finances, and was expecting more affluence in the future.

I was pleased to have met him, and wanted him to be my friend, and perhaps a business partner in years to come. He was intelligent and enterprising. Best of all he was not tied down with a family of his own with responsibilities and restrictions. I walked down with him to his auto rickshaw. We drove down to the Connaught Place for a meal. We did not approach the glitzy restaurants, but headed for a way side stall. The food was tasty wholesome filling and cheap. Shamim had to hand over the auto rickshaw to his friend Arif for the night shift. We parted, and I walked back to my hotel.

I stood outside the building and stared at the neon sign. The three storey building with twenty five guest rooms was not an imposing structure. It merged with the surrounding buildings; the glare of the neon light was the only indication that it was a hotel. There were a few other hotels on the street, and since these were fairly close to Connaught Place and the railway station, business was good. The tariff was very reasonable and affordable for the common man. Very rarely did the hotel get any advance booking, occasionally from old patrons. The clientele were mostly off the street, or brought in by auto rickshaw and taxi drivers for a small commission from the hotel.

I looked at my wristwatch. The time was nearly ten thirty, yet the street looked fairly busy. Taxis, auto rickshaws and jostling pedestrians were weaving their way, and did not appear to be thinning down. There were moments of emptiness, only to be crowded again with the next wave of traffic as the lights changed. In one such lull in the traffic I heard raised voices behind me, and saw a man in expensive clothes addressing a well dressed lady in abusive language, and was even gesturing to strike her. The language and the behaviour did not match the clothes and the appearances. I intervened. Initially the man tried to ignore me as I approached them.

"What's going on?" I enquired.

"None of your damn business, get lost!" The man shouted.

"I'll make it my business if you do not explain," I threatened.

"She is a whore, and owes me some money. Now get lost!" He said belligerently.

"You are standing in front of my hotel and making a scene," I said. "It makes no difference to me what she is. You are giving this neighbourhood a bad reputation. Unless you calm down right away, I am going to call the police." The mention of police seemed to have a soothing effect.

"I have paid him his due." The girl said. She appeared fairly young, may be in her early twenties. "He wants to take all my earnings. I shall be much obliged if you do call the police. He is threatening to beat me."

"I can't solve your problems," I said, "But if you don't want to go with him, there is no reason why you should." I turned to the man and said, "You better beat it before I call the police. They will arrest both of you, and you will have to pay whatever money you took from the girl and more, to bribe your way out of jail."

By this time the man had calmed down, and realised that he was not going to be able brow-beat her, and made a hasty retreat, muttering threats beneath his breath.

"Well you can go home, now that the man has gone." I told her.

"Do you own this hotel?" She asked, unable to resist her feminine curiosity.

"No I am only the night manager."

"I am a call girl, and work mainly as escorts of business guests. I don't know what prompted me to listen to that man. I had met him once in a five star hotel, in company of someone I trust."

I looked at her closely. She was younger than I initially thought and pretty. She was about five feet four inches in height, slim with a good figure, accentuated by the body hugging sari she was wearing. The light was insufficient to she details of her attire. A pert upturned nose in an oval face framed by dark curly long hair plaited at the back looked at me through large bright dark intelligent eyes with long lashes. "Well if you will excuse me, I have to start my shift and take over from the day manager. She must be clock-watching and wondering where I was. Also if we keep chatting on the pavement at this time of the night, the police will definitely arrest us."

"I am Shyamali. What is your name?"

"Amar," I said.

"Will you meet me tomorrow at that restaurant?" She asked, pointing to a coffee house a hundred metres down the street. "Say at five in the evening.

"O.K," I was curious. "But you won't get any business through me," I rejoined.

"Sometimes it is nice to be able to talk to someone other than a client," She laughed. She had white even teeth and a pleasant peel to her laughter. I waved her off, and watched her walking down the poorly lighted road towards the nearest bus stop: her heels clicking on the stone flagged pavement, fading with the distance. She was swallowed by the gathering gloom. I turned and stepped into the brightness of the hotel foyer. The security man was seated near the reception. He waved at me and I smiled. In the manager's room Sunita was impatiently waiting for me. She gave me a quick rundown of our guests, and wished me goodnight. Her car was parked at the back of the hotel, a blue 'Maruti 800'. She lived with her parents at Vasant kunj since her divorce a couple of years ago.

I looked at my watch. It was ten minutes past five, and I had been sipping my first cup of coffee for the past fifteen minutes. I decided to wait another five minutes for Shaymali to come. May be she has forgotten, or got called away on business, I thought. I opened the evening edition of the local news paper and glanced through the headlines. There was nothing to catch the eye. The same political mud slinging and scandals of the show biz and controversies regarding selection of the Indian cricket team due to go to Australia dominated the print media. The inside pages reported a murder and one conviction of rape. There was an interesting article about spontaneous appearance of ash on the framed photographs of Sai Baba, one of the popular God-men of the country. I kept glancing through the large window next to my table in the hope of catching a glimpse of Shaymali before she arrives. I missed her.

A shadow fell on my paper and I looked up to see her smiling at me. She removed the shoulder strap of her purse and put it on the table, before sitting down across from me. For a moment I did not recognise her. She was a totally different person. Instead of the stylish dress and hairdo and sophisticated make up the girl in front of me was in tight jeans and a loose cotton blouse. Her hair was free from all restraints and as she shook off the few errant strands that threatened to obscure her vision, she painted a picture of confidence and careless elegance.

"I had given up on you and was about to leave. I thought you stood me up." I said.

"I'm sorry, the traffic held me up, or rather the buses were too crowded, and I had to let two of them go before I could squeeze myself into the third one. I chose the wrong time of the day to meet you and was swamped by the homeward bound crowd," She apologised. "I was afraid that you wouldn't come.

"Well, here I am. What did you want to talk about? I asked mirroring her smile. I waved at the waitress and asked for two more cups of coffee. "Do you want to eat anything?" I asked turning to look back at her. "I was going to order a chicken roll for myself; feeling a bit peckish."

"No, just coffee is fine, thank you." She said pulling up a chair. "It is not often I meet a person who goes out of his way to help someone in an awkward situation. I thought I should like to know you better, and cultivate your friendship."

"If you are serious about getting to know each other, then I think it's only fair that you should start by telling me a bit about yourself," I said leaning back on my chair.

Over coffee Shayamali said, "I am a commercial artist with a degree in fine arts, and do freelance work with a few advertising companies."

I was surprised to say the least. "How do you explain your second profession?" I asked.

"It's a long story," She said. "As a commercial artist I often meet customers in five star hotel conference rooms and the lobbies to discuss their needs. I also get invited to many company dinners and cocktail parties. The marketing managers do all the bargaining and hard selling. I have to be there to look into the feasibility aspect of the projects, and cost implications. I have to make rough sketches sometimes to understand what the customers want from us, how they want us to project their products or company and also which segment of the market the ad will be aimed at. Like a consultant of sort."

"I became familiar with a few hotel managers, and was on first name basis with some. One night in a party when I was alone, I was approached by a hotel manager with the proposal to work as an escort or a call girl. He painted a very rosy picture. I was offended, and told him off. I left the party early, and made it a point never to visit that hotel again."

"Life has a way of mocking us, make us eat our words. A few months later my father had a heart attack, and was taken urgently to a private hospital. He was put in the intensive care and looked very pale. He was sweating profusely and taking shallow rapid breaths. His eyes were closed. I knew the morphine had eased his pain, but I was scared for him. He looked close to death. He had an angiogram next morning, and we were told that his coronary arteries were clogged. He needed cardiac bypass surgery as soon as possible. The hospital quoted a sum of money for the procedure and stay in the hospital which was way beyond our means. I did not know anyone who would be willing to loan me that amount. That night I realised how flimsy the fabric of our society is. We have no security. If a family member falls ill or if the bread-earner looses his or her job, the whole family stares at starvation and homelessness. I vowed to myself that I'll never be in that situation ever again. I wanted to build insulation around us with money."

"I sat alone in my room for a long time, and then out of sheer desperation I visited that hotel manager. He heard me out, and agreed to arrange the money for me provided I consented to come in at short notice to his and a few other hotels to act as escorts for patrons, mostly elderly businessmen and senior executives. I had to entertain them and be prepared to have sex if the client so chose. I had very little choice. I agreed. My father recovered and came home after a month in the hospital. He is not aware. He would have preferred to have died than subject me to such humiliation. It was entirely my choice."

"These hotels have many rich clients who are too busy jetting around to spend time at home with their families. For varied reason they seem to relish combining business with pleasure and seek the company of beautiful young girls. They are successful and generous, willing to spend money for a good time."

"Yesterday when you met me, I was in a very awkward situation. Normally I do not meet anyone outside those few hotels. There is security and anonymity. That man was a friend of one of the managers, and though I did not know him well, I did not anticipate any problem. That was a case of serious misjudgement."

"Why are the hotel managers interested in acting as pimps? I asked.

"Two reasons, I believe: firstly to hold on to the rich clients, and secondly for the handsome commission."

"How long have you been in the sex trade?"

"About two years. I have paid up most of my debts. We have moved to a bigger apartment, and another year should see me comfortably off. I don't think I can carry on like this for long without my colleagues or family finding out. My job as a free lance artist and consultant status helps to explain the erratic hours. I try to camouflage myself as much as possible to avoid detection."

"Yes I can see that. I barely recognised you when you pulled that chair."

We sat silent for some time staring at the passing traffic not knowing what to say.

"It's your turn now Amar. You know more about me than anyone else; time to reciprocate." She grinned at me.

"I'm afraid there is very little to tell." I murmured. Then with a smile I explained to her, "I had an accident five years ago in Dev Prayag. I was found on the river bank by Anand, a sage, and he cared for me. I was in and out of consciousness for nearly a month, and then took another month to recover my strength. You see, I have lost all my memory prior to that accident. I do not know who I am or what I was doing in Dev Prayag. I do not know if I have any family or friends. After I recovered, we went on a pilgrimage, a long trek over the beautiful but barren glaciers and ranges of the Himalayas. I have never breathed such pure air and never felt such quiet and tranquillity. Once we returned I advertised in the local and a national paper, but did not get any response. Anand was a scholar, and was a senior civil servant before he renounced the world. He taught me many things. That winter he urged me to go back to civilisation. I worked in a small family hotel in Hardwar for some time before coming to Delhi. I think I'll build my own hotel one day, though how I am going to do that I do not know yet."

"Do you not wonder about your family?"

"Yes I do, but I do not know what to do about it. I don't even know which town or city I belong to, where to start my search."

"Well at least you don't have to worry about others for now."

"True, but it is a very lonely existence. If I had not spent time with Anand, I might have gone out of my mind. He taught me to live for the moment, and to meditate. It does bring mental balance and peace."

"If you don't mind my company I would like to lighten your loneliness. I also need some one with whom I can talk freely, without having to tell half truths, not having to worry about revealing my secrets."

"Here's my mobile telephone number. Give me a ring when you need me. I am free most days. I work at night remember? I do go to the library from time to time, and roam the city in search of inspiration and ideas to make my fortune."

The autumn day was drawing to a close. Street lights were fighting for supremacy over the fading Sun. Humming mosquitoes found our unprotected ankles. It was time for me to report for duty. As if on cue we got up from our chairs and laughed. I paid the bill and escorted Shyamali to the nearest bus stop. We chatted till her bus departed taking her away. I traced my steps towards the familiar street and the hotel entrance.

Months passed. I settled into a rhythm: cat naps during the night, some sleep in the morning, the day spent either in the library or roaming the air-conditioned shopping malls in the 'Connaught Circus area to evade the sweltering heat. Life was passing me by. I could feel the throb of excitement and wealth around me and knew that opportunity was calling me to grab it with both hands and ride it. I could not make up my mind which way to go. I was restless. I had been networking with local traders and other hoteliers. I was looking for an opening to plunge in.

Sunday afternoons were special. Shyamali, Shamim, Arif and I met for lunch and chit-chat. The only time we could spare for some friendly gossip and catch-up. All of us were eager to progress in life: none of us were going anywhere. Shamim's mother was not keeping well. Arif's shanty town was knee deep in filthy sewage following the predictable monsoon downpour. Shyamali was not making much headway with her insulation policy. Our sense of kinship and solidarity deepened. We learnt to trust and understand each other better.

One Sunday evening I was off. Shyamali stayed back after lunch to keep me company. She did not have much on hand, and we decided to go for a movie, and then dinner. We came back to my room. The day was spent in easy companionship and we were in a light hearted flirty mood. We were sitting on the sofa, and the closeness made us aware of each other. I put my arm around her, and she snuggled up to me, resting her head on my shoulder. She gazed at me and I gently traced my index finger along her jaw. She laughed and pulled my head down for a quick kiss, which turned into lingering moist warmth of an experience. She was quite experienced, and guided me with her tongue.

I have not had much luck with grown women since my accident, and any previous experience was wiped clean off my memory. Shyness was holding me back, but my heart was pounding, and I could feel an erection developing. Shyamali also felt my erection, and took her lips off mine to speak:

"Amar, do you know I have never had any relationship. Any kiss or sex I had was only with clients, to give them pleasure, never to pleasure me. Would you take me please?"

She sounded wistful and hesitant. I looked into her pleading eyes, and thought why not? I was as eager for sex as she was. There was no gentleness in what followed. We practically tore our clothes off each other, and the frenzy of youth took over as it boiled over us in a tangle of limbs and desire.

Eventually spent and sweating we lay limp in each others arms to catch our breath. Later we had a more gentle and enduring sex. I never realised it could be so exhilarating, so satisfying and leave me so contented. I escorted Shyamali to her bus and wistfully watched it spew diesel fumes at me before merging into the unending stream of traffic.

We knew that we were not in love with each other, but were captive of the moment and desire. Our relationship fulfilled a longing for companionship, a need for sexual expression. Over the months that followed, we met may be once a month, and spent the evenings in each others company, ending up in each others arms in my bed to release our pent up desires. Shyamali never spent the night with me. She wanted to preserve the illusion of a working artist at home. Shamim and Arif did not know and did not suspect our liaison. We were happy to keep it that way.

One afternoon I was gazing at the displays in a polished shop window at Connaught place. There was a lull in the heat of the afternoon amongst the shoppers, a noticeable thinning of the crowd. I was in the deep shadows thrown by the overhanging terrace supported by circular white columns enclosing the pavement, enjoying the opulence and the ambience as I walked slowly, aimlessly killing time, rubbing shoulders with the super rich. I saw the reflection of some one calling me. He came closer and slapped my back:

"Rajiv! Of all people, where have you been hiding yourself?" He asked.

I turned around, a bit puzzled. "Are you talking to me?" I asked. I knew it was a silly question to ask, since my back was still smarting from his enthusiastic slapping.

"What do you mean? Do you see anyone between us, or are you trying to be funny?" Then looking at the puzzled expression on my face, he asked softly, "Don't you recognise me?"

"Did you call me Rajiv? I asked not answering his question.

"That's your name isn't it," Was his smiling rejoinder.

"I don't know," I said. "How do you know me, and are you sure you got the right person?"

"Yes I have got the right person unless you are a ghost. I have known you since my childhood until you disappeared five years ago. As far as I know you do not have any twins."

"I am called Amar, and I wouldn't know about a twin."

"You are talking in riddles. What's wrong with you? Stop pulling my leg, if that's what you are doing. I have had enough of your practical jokes."

"No it's not a practical joke. I had an accident five years ago, and lost my memory. I have no recollection of the past."

"Now that is strange, and would explain not having heard from you for such a long time. What are you doing now? Can you come home with me to meet my dad? He will be thrilled to see you."

"I am working as a night manager in a small hotel, and have to report for work at six O'clock this evening when I start my shift."

"That does not leave enough time for the round trip. I am Vijay, by the way. Let's sit down and have some 'Lassi' (a yoghurt drink) while we fill each other on events and gossips." He said pointing at a small cafe within the circle of the green island across the road.

We crossed the road and walked on the grassy knoll up to the cafe, and pulled up a chair each under the shade of the umbrella strategically placed. A waiter saw us and came over to take our orders.

"Two sweet lassi," Vijay said loudly even before the waiter reached our table. "With lot of ice," was his rejoinder. "Well, where were we?" He continued.

"You do the talking and fill me up first. I don't have much to say," I replied.

The traffic island at the Connaught circus in quite extensive, almost in the shape of two joined up circles, with an underground air-conditioned shopping complex 'Palika Bazar' under one of the circles. The roads radiate out like rays of the Sun from the green circles in various directions cutting through the concentric circles of shopping arcades with white colonnades that lay hugging the roads separating them and the green circles.

"Our dads were close friends and colleagues, professors at the Delhi University. We lived in the campus and were next door neighbours. You were the only child of you parents, but I have an elder sister who is now married and lives in Mumbai. We are of the same age, and went to school together. Later you were selected in the competitive examination to the Indian Institute of Technology at Kanpur to study mechanical engineering. I joined St. Stephens, and did economics honours here in Delhi. At present I am the manager at State Bank of India, Moti-bagh branch. My father has retired. We live in a flat at Moti-Bagh, and I am not married."

"When you were in your second year at the engineering college, your parents were involved in a car crash. Both died on the spot. My dad rang you at your hostel, and asked you to come over. You stayed with us for the duration of your parents' last rites, and then one night you left a note for my dad explaining you needed a change of scene, and disappeared. He advertised in various papers in the missing persons section, and got the police involved without much success."

He paused and we looked at each other in contemplative silence for some time. Then he said, "It's your turn now."

"What you have just said is all new to me. I do not remember any of it. I do not have any recollection of my life prior to the accident. It's like I was born a fully grown man, with no childhood or adolescence. The only memory that haunts me most nights is the face of a young girl crying in pain and calling for help. And then I find myself falling through darkness. I wake up bathed in sweat and gripped with terror. I used to have this night mare every night in the past, but now the frequency is much less. I assume that would be the reliving of my accident, but I cannot recollect either the name of the girl, or my relationship with her."

"What I do remember is short and simple. I woke up in a hermitage at Dev Prayag. It took me months to recover fully. I spent a year with Anand, who found me by the river bank and nursed me through my fever and delirium. Not only did I have severe head injury, I had also developed hypothermia and pneumonia from exposure to the ice-cold water. In the summer of that year I accompanied him and other 'sadhus' on a pilgrimage, walking over the Gomukh glacier and through some beautiful barren and spectacular land well above the tree line in the Himalayas. We visited Kedarnath, and then climbed down to Badrinath and Joshimath before returning to Dev Prayag. The crisp unpolluted rarefied air of the high mountain ranges helped me to regain my strength. I then went to Hardwar and graduated with commerce. I worked in a hotel during that time to sustain myself. I came to Delhi a little over a year ago, and landed this job as the night manager of a small hotel near the railway station. I am looking for an opening to start my own business."

Silently we appraised each other. My mind was in a whirl churning and digesting the information I just received. "Are you sure you are talking to the right person?" I asked. "I do not remember anything you just said."

"I have known you for more than fifteen years," Vijay said seriously. "I am quite sure. We grew up like brothers, and were close friends."

My thoughts were chaotic, flitting from one thought to the other. "Do I have any blood relations?" I asked

"I don't know," was his reply. "Why don't you come home and talk to dad. Both my parents will be overjoyed to see you alive and well. He will be able to answer most of your questions. Also there is some money due to you from your parents' life insurance policies. He was the executor of your father's will."

I remained silent and pensive for a while. Dusk was settling around us. The crowd changed. Families with children disappeared to be replaced by young adults. Shrill voices of the very young changed to trilling laughter of excited teenage girls on the brink of adulthood and young women, engrossed in their own world and rosy dreams. The cars and buses had switched on their headlights; bizarre shadows chased each other round the circle and across it. Some of the vendors were closing their stalls. Eddies of cool breeze sprung up, providing a refreshing feel to the end of the day.

"I can't come now. I start work soon. What about the weekend, Sunday perhaps?"

"That will be great! Come over by eleven in the morning and have lunch with us. That way you will have most of the day to trawl through your past and get answers to your questions. As I said my parents will be thrilled to have you." Vijay gave me his address and telephone number. We parted. I made my way back to the hotel. My mind was trying to sift through all the new information, going round and round, trying to fit the familiar face of the unknown girl. Before I realised, I found myself standing in front of the hotel.

I walked behind the reception counter and took over from Sunita. It was a busy evening, keeping me on my toes. Later that night when the lobby was deserted, and the occupants were asleep in their beds my mind returned to nibble at the amazing revelations I heard that afternoon. I was not Amar, but Rajiv! Am I the same person I was before the accident? Have the knock on my head changed my behaviour, my thinking, my character? When I meet people who knew me before the accident, will they notice a difference in me? Above all I hoped that the mystery of my nightmares, especially the identity of the girl in my dreams will be revealed. The week passed slowly. To my fevered mind Sunday seemed to take a long time coming. Shamim had dropped in one evening and I asked him to tell the others that I won't be coming to the Sunday lunch at our usual place. I did not tell him about Vijay or what he said. I wanted to digest the truth first, and let my mind reconcile with the facts before telling the others. I thought I'll wait another week and tell the others after I had spoken to Vijay's dad. What's his name? I wish I could remember.

At last I woke up to a bright and sunny Sunday morning. I was dressed and ready much before time. I looked at my watch for the fifteenth time. Though the watch was ticking and the second's needle was moving as it should, time seemed to stay still. Fed up of clock watching, I took to the road, the heat of the morning Sun was not unpleasant. A bus took me to Moti Bagh. Vijay's dad had bought the flat after retirement. I had no difficulty in finding the address, and rang the bell an hour before the scheduled time.

Vijay opened the door and with a shout of excitement rushed to welcome me with an embrace. His parents heard him, and came out of their rooms. I smiled at them, and touched their feet as is the custom to greet elders in the family. They in turn gave me a tight hug, followed by close scrutiny at arms length and finally the declaration that I have not changed much just matured from a boy to a man. We entered the lounge and made ourselves comfortable. For a moment we were all at a loss for words. The room was spacious, uncluttered and tastefully decorated. A couple of oil paintings adorned the wall behind me, and a book shelf formed part of the wall in front of me. A large glass top coffee table was placed in the centre of the room. The white marble floor was cool and pleasant. A ceiling fan was circling, trying hard to neutralise the heat and humidity. An air conditioner stood to one side waiting for the day to become even hotter. A couple of doors led off on my right, probably to the kitchen and the bedrooms. The visitors' toilet was next to the entrance hall.

Vijay's dad was tall, nearly six feet in height and of slim built with a little stoop. A mop of silver hair covered his scalp. He wore a pair of metal rimmed glasses, and had the day's newspaper in his left hand. It was obvious that my arrival had interrupted his reading, and he forgot to take off the reading glasses. He was more than sixty years of age, but looked good for his age. He wore starched white kurta and 'Aligarhi'. Vijay's mother on the other hand was of slight built and of medium height. Her long black waist length hair, streaked generously with silver was hanging loose. It was moist, again my arrival robbed her the time to dry her hair, parted in the centre, a red streak of vermillion highlighting the parting. She was wearing a white sari with red border. She looked serene and happy. She went back into the kitchen and came out after a little while with a cup of hot tea and some snacks which she placed in front of me.

"We have just had our breakfast: please help yourself," she said.

"I understand that you have lost your memory in an accident and do not remember anything from the past?" Vijay's dad asked.

"Yes," I said softly. "I don't seem to remember anything prior to the accident I had five years ago."

"I am Jayant, Vijay's dad, and that's my wife Jaya. You have already met Vijay. Vijay must have told you that your parents were very close friends of ours. We have known you since your birth. You have spent many hours at our previous house in the university campus, growing up together with Vijay. We were your next door neighbours. You two went to the same school and were inseparable until you joined IIT Kanpur."

"I came today to learn about my past and rediscover myself." I said. "I came to listen to you and find out about my parents, my ancestry and if I have any blood relations. I shall be grateful for whatever you can tell me about my parents and myself."

"Your father was the youngest son of four brothers and two sisters." Jayant said. "Your ancestral home was in Asansol, near Kolkata, though I do not know the address. Your mother had a sister much younger, and was in primary school when your parents got married. Your parents met each other during their college days in Kolkata, and fell in love. They married against the wishes of both sets of parents and were estranged from their families. They had very little contact with their families, and were very happy with each other. I think one of your father's sisters visited your parents once when you were in the engineering college at Kanpur. Your parents did not discuss the visit with us. The others however never bothered to maintain contact, and the attitude was reciprocated by your parents."

"You are the only child. You were intelligent and good academically as well as in sports, a popular figure in your school and college, elected the school captain in your final year. You did well in the competitive examinations, and received offer of placement from a number of good institutions. You chose IIT Kanpur, deciding on mechanical engineering. You were in your second year at IIT when your parents had a fatal car crash. I called you back. Understandably you were shell shocked, and after the last rites was over, one evening you left a note for me in my study and walked out of our house. We tried to trace you through the newspapers and reported to the police without much success. You can imagine how thrilled and excited we were when Vijay told us that he met you accidentally at Connaught Circus. It was almost miraculous. We had practically given up hope of ever finding you. To see you now sitting in front of us, safe and sound is like a dream."

"There are some other issues that had me in a dilemma. Your parents had life insurance policies, and made me the executor of their will. Your disappearance put me on the spot, and did not know what to do with the money, and was in two minds to try and contact your uncles. Eventually I decided to wait for seven years before taking that step, and am I glad that you surfaced! Imagine what a mess it would have been if I had handed the money over to your uncles and aunts."

I left after a sumptuous lunch and reviving the past. Vijay gave me a list of my friends who were in Delhi and had been asking about me. Some were my school friends and others were from my engineering college. They were apparently quite keen to get in touch with me. Vijay had rung them to inform them of my present whereabouts.

Over the next week or two I did just that, ringing around and networking: reviving old contacts, letting them fill me in with anecdotes and incidents from the past, trying to jog my memory. I even managed to meet a few of them over the weekends. Akash was my room mate at Kanpur and was studying architecture. He had joined a reputed architectural firm in Delhi and doing well for himself. Fernando, a civil engineer, has his own construction company. Sudhir was into computer software, doing freelance work. Everyone was sympathetic, understanding and accommodating, willing to overlook my lapses, trying to rekindle my memory by supplying nuggets of information and snippets of gossip from our student days. Gradually I began to piece together my past. The girl in my dream still eluded me. None of my friends knew of her.

Arif lived in a slum near the Inter State Bus Terminal. Nearly three hundred families lived there. The houses were typical of many shanty towns dotted around Delhi and other big cities of India. They were constructed of bamboo frames, corrugated tin and plywood, covered with tarpaulin or plastic sheets to make the roofs and walls watertight. The concept of drainage was non-existent and hygiene took a back seat in their daily struggle for survival.

Being close to the national highway, the land had suddenly acquired importance and land prices in that area sky rocketed. One of the local unscrupulous construction companies was trying to evict the residents by force and buy it cheap from the Delhi administration who owned the land. They were trying to project the land as inhabitable rocky wasteland. Their aim was to develop a large shopping complex. The residents were squatters, and had been living on that land for decades. They had squatters right, and any kind of eviction entitled them to alternative accommodation. The company on the other hand had money and high political connections, not to mention hired thugs who were harassing the residents, and had even assaulted a few. The local police had been bribed and were looking the other way.

Taking the matter to the law courts seemed the most logical option, but there was a dilemma. Normally civil cases can take up to twenty years for a resolution, a fact in favour of the residents, but if the magistrate could be bribed, they would loose the case within a year. Legal challenge was an expensive and exhausting affair, and not many dare to embark on that route. The outcome was unpredictable, and not for the less affluent masses in the Indian society. The uncertainty of the future of their families was wearing the residents down. They were angry and upset and frustrated. They were unsure of what to do. A few families who had the means and lacked the stomach to fight, moved away from the area either buying or renting apartments elsewhere in the city.

"Can you describe the residents: what kind of people are they?" I asked Arif one day. "Do they have steady income, or are they just beggars and pickpockets?"

"Every one of them is self employed with families. They have diverse interests, and earn enough to live within their means. They do not have huge savings to put down as deposits for the new apartments. There are small shopkeepers, middlemen living on commissions, carpenters, masons, taxi drivers; some are bank and government office clerks. Others have small businesses like mine."

"Are they willing to spend money to retain their hold on the land, or put in hard work?" I asked. A germ of an idea was sprouting at the back of my mind.

"I am sure they will, if they believe in the project and have confidence in achieving their objective. They need a solid plan and good leadership. They will also need financial support." Arif paused and then added, "What are you getting at?"

"I have an idea, but I need to think deeper. You said that the company has persuaded Delhi administration to sell the land by auction through sealed tenders. Is that correct?"

"Yes as far as I know, though the date has not been fixed yet. The company will try to muscle out any competition and bid low. They know the big construction companies do not want to buy land with squatters, spending half a lifetime fighting in the courts, and providing fertile ground for opposition political parties to run a media circus at their expense."

"I was thinking that if we do not make our intentions known until the last minute, and then put up a front man who can't be traced back to us, we may out-bid the company. Of course we have to ensure that the auction is not rigged. A tall order I know, and that is why I need to think. I need to talk with the others and pick their brains. I'll also try to pull in a few favours that people owe me. Let's meet next Sunday at lunch time. By then I'll have a plan. I need to know our strength before talking to some of the residents and raise their hopes. We cannot afford any leak from our side. We have to plan carefully and put up some money for the deposit if we are to bid. I would also like to know what kind of help we can expect from the residents."

"It will be a challenge to keep the plan a secret once the residents are told," Shamim mused. He had been quiet for a while, and listening to our conversation. "I think we have to create a core group amongst the residents, whom we trust explicitly. They will be aware of the whole plan, and will tell the others on a need to know basis."

"That's good thinking, and the kind of talk I like; but if the company finds out about it, they will play rough." Arif said.

"Can you not organise a civil defence group from the residents, who will patrol the area at night and be vigilant of attacks from thugs hired by the company? They have to be especially careful about arson. Starting a fire in a slum is the easiest thing to do, and that will destroy any evidence of habitation on the land. Of course people will have to take turns, as everyone has a business to run and offices to go to during the day." I remarked. "Let the patrolling group carry 'lathis', and large metal torches. They are good as weapons, but are not illegal to carry."

"We hadn't thought of it that way. I think what you say is very relevant, and I must mobilise able bodied men and some of the women to create our own protection force," Arif replied. "Even if the police is informed, they will not be on the scene for the first half hour at least."

"Try to get some sand and keep it handy, and arrange storage for water in case you do have to fight fire. Be prepared for all eventualities." I said. "And Arif, make sure that the residents put up a united front at all cost. There should not be any division based on caste, religion or trade."

"I better get going. You have given me a lot to chew on and to act quickly. I'll see you next Sunday as usual then. Bye" Arif left.

We were silent for some time, each chasing our own thoughts. "The plan is good but very risky and audacious" Shamim said at last breaking the silence.

"If we want to get rich, we have to take a plunge and this seems to be an opportunity not to be missed. I know it is easy for me to risk everything on this venture as I have no dependents. It will be very different for you, Shyamali, Vijay and others whom I'll try to rope in. Arif and the residents have a stake in this fight and should be easy to persuade." I said.

"Moreover we lack experience in construction work, management at that scale and the finances." Shamim argued.

"I have thought of the challenges ahead, and I plan to rope in a few of my friends who have the required experience. Some people owe me a few favours. These people are well positioned to help us. Only problem is will they remember me?" I paused to think.

"You know that Akash is an architect and a partner in a reputed construction company. He can recommend and guide us in the initial stages. Vijay is a branch manager of the State bank in Moti Bagh, and should be able to help us with our loan application and be the guarantor. Ranjit's sister is PA to the Lieutenant Governor of Delhi, and I am sure I'll be able to exert some political pressure through her help."

"Who's Ranjit? I don't think I know him." Shamim said.

"He was with Vijay and me in school. I understand we were close friends. His father was an accountant for the university and lived in the campus and was our neighbour."

"You seem to have useful friends." Shamim laughed.

"I hope they will remain friends when I start asking favours." I replied. "I intend to entice them all into this project and be shareholders of our company. That way they will have self interest in the project and will see it through. It will also mitigate our financial situation to some extent."

"What kind of returns do you anticipate?" Shamim asked.

"I honestly don't know at this moment of time, but I am going to study the whole plan with Akash and Vijay. Between them they should be able to fill me in enough to get a rough idea. I am also hoping that they will pull in their contacts."

Twelve of us met that Sunday afternoon at our usual place. I presented my plan to the group: "Look, here is a chance to get hold of prime land at an affordable price. If we develop a residential complex of one two and three bedroom apartments, it is possible to provide all the residents of the slum with free flats, and make a substantial profit for ourselves. It will serve two purposes. Firstly the residents will not be harassed by the thugs and their children will have a healthy environment to grow up. Secondly if we make a profit, we will create a financially viable company and the experience will be invaluable."

"It is a huge and costly undertaking," Shamim said. "Do we have that kind of money to gamble?"

"Vijay and Akash have done a preliminary costing. They had gone to the site with Arif, and worked out the number of dwellings that can be constructed, costs involved, and the range of potential profit. I would like you all to look through their report. Each of you will have to decide for yourself, and live with the decision. I do not want us blaming each other. We will form a registered company and all of us will be shareholders depending on our investments in terms of money and time plus effort. Those of us who will contribute in professional capacity will record their fee that the company would owe them, and they will be given shares in lieu. That goes for Akash as the Architect, Arif as labour manager, Shamim as logistics manager and Shyamali looking after advertisement including printing of brochures. Ranjit can be the in-house book-keeper. I'll look for a good legal team and I want you all to pull in your political contacts to help smooth the path through planning permission and other bureaucratic impediments. We should meet regularly and keep in contact on a daily basis to update each other."

"It looks like a very exciting project, but will involve a lot of hard work and frustration." Shyamali commented.

"We need to raise enough money to secure the land and to start the construction process. Completion will depend on instalment payments from new buyers," Vijay stated. "According to Akash we can build ten star shaped towers of one hundred and twenty flats in each tower with lifts and fire escapes over six floors. The basement will be car parks and shops. The towers will be arranged in a circle and in the centre we can build a community centre, club, gym etc. depending on demand. Three hundred of the apartments will be for the residents, and the other nine hundred will be for sale to the general public. I estimate that once we sell all the apartments, we will make a substantial profit. The details are in the report. There should be a high demand for these apartments."

We talked well into the night. Good thing I had taken the evening off. We discussed various scenarios, including going bust. We eventually came back to the problem of securing the land.

"I am going to speak to a media person to highlight the problem of the residents, and try to build political pressure firstly to stop the auction being rigged, and secondly stopping any commercial development. I do not know if he will help me or not, but lets take one step at a time."

"Arif, do you know any one in the corporation office who can tip us off when the auction date is going to be announced?" I asked, "I don't want to start the media circus too soon. It may loose its impact if the timing is not right."

"One of the residents works in the corporation office as a clerk," Arif replied. "I'll ask him to let us know in time." He paused for a moment and added, "I have to go now. I am working tonight"

We dispersed. Excitement and anticipation gave added spring to our steps. Now that we have committed ourselves, there was no turning back. All were eager to join, and agreed to entice others to buy our shares. We had to get the money to start us off. We all had some put by, but none of us was rich. I left the buzz of receding voices and made my way to my hotel room. I could not sleep too much adrenaline in the blood. I sat down with a pad and a pen to write down the minutes of the first general body meeting of 'Kohinoor enterprise', a name we agreed on for our new company.

I had made a list of my contacts, and that week I went about meeting them, trying to enlist their help. First on my list was Mr Suresh Sharma, owner of a string of newspapers and magazines, well connected and respected. He was a very busy man. It was with some trepidation that I had rung his secretary for an appointment. Recalling his reluctance and later embarrassment at having to borrow money from me, I was not sure that he would want to see me. I was pleasantly surprised when his secretary rang back half an hour later asking me if I could see him that afternoon. I was punctual, and was directed to his office by the receptionist. As I entered his office, he came round his bureau and shook my hand in a firm grip.

"So, what can I do for you young man? A flicker of a smile softened his stern features. He was my height, wiry and alive like a coiled panther ready to jump. Metal rimmed glasses gave his eyes an unusual lustre and a penetrative quality I have not often encountered. His hairs were snow white and thinning above a broad lined forehead, testament to his age. "Take a seat," He said pointing to an executive chair on the visitor's side of the bureau.

I sat down and hesitantly started, "I need your help." He waited expectantly. "There is a slum near the Inter Stat Bus Terminus, home to three hundred families. Most of them have small businesses and trades; some are salaried employee. An unscrupulous construction company with strong political connections has convinced the municipal corporation that the area is a wasteland, of no use to anyone, and wants to buy it cheap. They plan to develop a commercial complex. The corporation has decided to hold an auction through sealed tenders. None of the big and reputed construction companies are interested to get into litigation with the residents. This company however has hired thugs to harass and assault the local residents hoping to scare them into leaving the area. Some families, who had the means to buy or rent elsewhere in the city, have moved out. "Some of the residents, a few of my friends and I want to put in a bid as well for a residential complex for the sake of the residents, most of whom will be shareholders in our company."

By the time I finished explaining he was smiling broadly at me and asked, "Do you think you can become a property developer?"

"I think so," I said. "We have details of our plan here in this folder with an estimate of the costs." I handed him the folder. "One of my friends is an architect, and is experienced in this line of work. We have the expertise in banking and accountancy, and labour should not be a big problem since many of the residents are trades people with contacts."

"O.K, leave this folder with me for now. I'll think over it and send out a reporter to study the situation. If what you have just told me about harassment of the residents is true, then I certainly will make a big story out of it. I'll get in touch with you soon. Give your contact number and email address to my secretary on your way out."

I started to thank him, but he stopped me saying: "This is the least I can do for you. Also I smell a good story that will increase my circulation. By helping you, I may be helping myself as well. I may even become one of your shareholders if your plan works out!"

I was overjoyed to get his support and felt as if I was walking in the air. I was eager to spread the good news to my fellow would be shareholders. But I still needed some more information and professional help.

Mr Naresh Gupta was a senior partner in a reputed law firm in New Delhi. I outlined my plan to him and said, "I need your help to establish our company. It will be a closed company with shareholders. I would like your firm to front us to bid for the land in the auction. I have another request, this time on a different matter. I wish to carry with me deeded papers for buying options on land or property. The name of the seller and the price should be left blank. I envisage having to buy at short notice, and need the time to arrange my finances. If I buy options for a month or even two weeks, I should be able to arrange to get the money."

"You seem to have put in a lot of thought behind your venture. Unfortunately I am a criminal lawyer, and do not deal in properties. However we have a junior partner, Rakesh Malhotra, a very bright chap. I think he will be ideal for your case, including fronting for the auction. He is not in the office today, but I'll arrange a meeting tomorrow. I'll call you later to confirm the time. I like your idea of buying options. It will tie up the seller, stopping him getting into negotiations with other buyers."

I thanked him, and after a few minutes of social chit chat left him to meet Shamim who had left a message for me to go to his house. His mother had recently become rather insistent for him to get married, and he needed my help to convince his mother that now is not the right time.

Winter had set in, and the short days appeared to skim quickly. A cold wave gripped northern India. A thick envelope of freezing smog had descended on New Delhi. Arif called me one mid January night,

"Can you come to our colony straight away?" He sounded very excited and agitated.

"Not really," I replied. "You know I am working, and I cannot hand over to anyone at this time of the night. What happened?"

"What you expected has come to pass. Five residents of our colony were bribed heavily by the construction company to set fire to their own houses, and let it spread to the rest of the houses. Fortunately our patrol team spotted the flames early and alerted us. We are fighting the fire now."

I thought for a moment, and then said "Don't extinguish the fire completely. Let it burn just contain it so that it does not spread. How's the wind?"

"There is not much wind, but they have used petrol to start the fire, and you know our houses are made of flammable materials. What's your plan?"

"Soak the surrounding huts with water, and use sand to damp down the fire. I'll see if I can get the media interested and get some mileage for our cause. Get some video pictures before the fire burns out. If we can get a confession from those who started the fire on camera and manage to implicate the construction company, then it will be great!"

"Be quick" Arif replied.

"Call the police and the fire service only after media presence." I warned, and disconnected the line.

I opened my diary to look up Mr Suresh Sharma's residential number, and dialled.

"Who is it?" A sleepy voice floated down the wire.

"Sorry to wake you up at this time Mr Sharma, I am Rajiv. You may remember I spoke to you about a slum whose residents were being harassed by a construction company . . ." I paused.

"Yes."

"Well, they have set fire to a few of the huts. Do you think your paper will be interested in covering the story?"

"I'll send someone right away. Give me the location again."

He hung up after noting down the address and directions. It was time for me to wait patiently and hope my plan works. I made a hot cup of coffee, and stretched on the sofa, putting my feet on the coffee table. I shut my eyes and was lost in contemplation.

I must have dozed off. The sky was getting lighter heralding the new day. Birds were leaving their nests and the traffic was limbering up for the daily congestion. I got up. I had a lot to do. A hot leisurely shower and a heavy breakfast put me in an optimistic mood. I switched on the television, and was surprised to see the arson attempt was covered in the early morning news. I changed channels, and all the news channels were carrying the story as breaking news. Video footage of the burning huts was being shown. The fire looked much bigger than the five sporadic burning huts that I expected to see. I was worried about losses and injuries. I wondered if the fire got out of control. The coverage was more extensive and damaging for the construction company than I had even dreamed of. Mr Suresh Sharma must have sent a full television crew, and the other channels were picking up from him.

I went down to the colony to meet Arif. After speaking to me, Arif and some of the other residents evacuated the huts around the fire and let them burn as well. Thus instead of five huts burning, there were more than fifty. The blaze was much bigger and more dramatic, though always under control. The huts were constructed of cheap materials, and they had heaped some more on the pile to make the fire burn longer. No one was hurt and no one sustained any significant loss.

The media coverage however created significant political pressure on the ruling government, especially when it became apparent that the corporation was trying to sell the land to developers and deprive the residents of their homes. The opposition parties and human rights groups blew it up for their own ends. In the end the corporation had to concede that they were wrong, and offered the land to the residents for permanent settlement for a nominal ground rent. We were overjoyed, and dashed to our drawing boards, hoping to get the planning permission to build the residential complex for the residents and make our profit before the media interest died down. Those were the beginning of busy days and nights for me. I gave up my job as hotel manager to take over as managing director of our company.

The media coverage had given us another advantage. Since the residents got the land at practically no cost, and the auction was called off, we saved a lot of money. Banks were willing to give us loan for building purposes based on the land as equity. We could not have had it any better. We planned to build nine hundred apartments, a supermarket, a gym and a small park. A running track would surround the estate inside the boundary wall. We were able to sell off-plan on a tiered payment schedule. There was a huge demand for apartments in that location, and we repaid the bank well before the project was even half way to completion.

Shamim walked into my office one afternoon and pulled up a chair and said,

"Do you want to speculate?"

"You appear quite excited," I replied.

"Today I picked up two passengers from the ministry of planning. They were discussing government plans to transform Gurgaon into a modern shopping and office complex, with tower blocks and shopping malls. I got the impression that the planning is in the final stages, and once approved, big multinationals will start acquiring land soon."

"What are we waiting for?" I said. Lets go and look up Gurgaon!"

We got in Shamim's auto-rickshaw and drove off. Vast stretches of arid land lay in front of us. The irrigation canal had dried up. There has been little rain this spring, and a few farmers we spoke to were not optimistic of a good crop for the year.

We spoke to a few land owners, and let them know that we were looking for land to build factories. One person seemed quite interested, and after haggling we came to an understanding. I was carrying the options certificates, and he was happy to sell us first option on his land of ten acres. We arranged a date, and met again in the presence of his lawyer and Rakesh Malhotra representing us. The option gave us a month to decide on the final purchase. The price was reasonable. Our directors approved of the plan, and we purchased the land.

We bought two other chunks of land before the news of government's development plan broke. The land price in Gurgaon soared overnight, and we were sitting in the middle of it. Several multinational companies approached us to buy our land. We had decided that we will only sell to those companies who would give us the construction contract. Our company ballooned, and we were working all the hours of day and night for the next two years. We became one of the biggest construction companies in the city. We were rich.

Akash had left his parent company to be with us full time. Shyamali took over the responsibilities of marketing director. Vijay was looking after our finances and Arif was in-charge of personnel. Shamim looked after transport and logistics. I retained the post of chief executive and managing director of our flourishing company. Shamim got married and our company bought the property where he had a rented apartment, demolished and rebuilt it with large luxury apartments with all modern amenities. I bought an apartment in the same building. Shamim had created a transport company, a sister concern, providing taxis and auto-rickshaws to unemployed youths on a partnership basis. Akash and Shyamali were getting inseparable. Having worked together on promoting our company for the past two years, they enhanced their initial mutual attraction to respect and affection. Everyone seemed to be settled and happy except myself. I was feeling restless and lonely. The girl in my nightmares still haunted me, and I was no closer to solving that mystery.

THE SINGER

Rini was staring at herself in the full length mirror of her opulent hotel room and adjusting her saree. She was getting ready for the evening. She looked at herself closely: eight long and eventful years had past since the fateful accident, eight years that transformed a bubbly young carefree girl into a matured sombre woman. Though she looked as beautiful and serene as ever her heart was scarred, her memory seared with personal losses.

Eight years ago she could not have even dreamt of today's reality. The passage of time had not been smooth, but Dadaji stood by her like a rock, providing her with strength, courage and confidence. He has aged. Rini smiled picturing his white haired wrinkled withered face in her mind. Earlier in the day she had gone shopping and bought a pashmina shawl for him. Dadaji was the most selfless person she has ever known, and true to form he was overwhelmed by the simple gift, and remonstrated with her for wasting money. Her eyes misted. Even her own father, whom she did not know, could not have done any more for her than Dadaji. She owed her success to him, and to her own hard work.

In those days of depression and self pity following the accident, after she was discharged from the hospital she cried incessantly and cursed her fate. She wished to die. Slowly the intensity of grief waned, and Shridhar Pandit introduced her to the world of Indian classical music. She drowned her sorrow and bitterness in the world of 'Sur' 'Tal' and 'Lai'. She practised for hours on end every day. An anxious Dadaji had to remind her of meal times and coax her to eat. Slowly but surely she grew in confidence and out of her melancholy. The dark depression dissipated. She started to take interest in the world around her. Over the months she learnt to use her artificial limb and at the end of the year could walk normally except for a slight limp. She could even run.

While in the orphanage, she had studied up to the tenth class, and the intervening years had made her rusty. At Shukra's insistence she joined evening classes for mature students. She passed the tenth and twelfth certificate examinations with good grades, and joined the local college. During the day she was busy with her music and studies, college and friends, housework and cooking. Her days were fully occupied, but her idle mind was invaded at night with nightmares, and memories flooded in. Occasionally she would wake up screaming, and Shukra came from his room to hold her and quieten her down. As time went by these episodes became less frequent, but the memory remained fresh, as if time had stood still.

Rini was laughing again, joking with her new friends. She never stayed out late her excuse was that she had to care for Shukra. At weekends she would join a few other girls to go to movies or even venture out on picnics. She tried to get over her fear of overhanging cliffs and heights. She succeeded in hiding her apprehensions from her friends.

History was her favourite subject. She dreamed of the characters, and their social systems. The heroism of the Rajputs and their women filled her with pride. She felt sad at the destruction of ancient Indian institutions and universities by invaders. She imagined herself living in those turbulent times, often to be caught unawares while day dreaming and brought back to reality by Shukra's voice calling her or clearing his throat to make his presence known with a gentle smile on his lips, reminding her it was meal time and that he was hungry.

Rini liked languages, but maths was not her forte. She had taken English and Hindi as her modern language subjects. She liked to write short stories and poetry. Especially the short couplets called 'shairi'. Over the years she would fill many diaries, and a few of them would form the lyrics of her songs.

She forged close friendship with two girls in her class, Rima and Rakhi. They were inseparable, and often referred to as the three 'R's. Though she shared in many gossips with her friends, she could not bring herself to discuss Rajiv or her accident. Those events seemed to have happened to her in a different life in another world. Her artificial leg of course was a constant reminder that it was not so. She had overcome the deep depression that had engulfed her, she still had a niche in her memory that she desperately tried to forget. As always happen, the more she tried to erase that memory, the more it would fill her head during hours of loneliness. She learnt to live with it, but still could not accept that Rajiv was no more. Her friends had no inkling of the dark secrets she was hiding from the world. To them Rini presented a smiling cheerful front, laughing and joking with them and sharing their gossip. Rini attracted a lot of attention from the boys, but was aloof to their interest. Her friends chided her from time to time, thinking she was too shy.

Rini sang in a couple of college functions and received acclaim for her voice quality. She had been training for four years, and Shridhar thought it was time to expose her to the public. He arranged an audition with the local radio station, which went well, and she sang a few times on the radio.

Rini liked to sing classical ragas. They have different moods and depths of feelings which appealed to her. Shridhar had discussed history of music and the evolution of 'Raga' music with her, to give her an insight into the world of classical music. Ancient civilisations had discovered music as a means to create emotionally pleasing effects through sound. It has evolved as a medium of expressing thought and feelings through tone and time. Indian music relies on one source of sound, like the voice or sitar, and is monophonic in nature. Western music on the other hand ensembles various instruments to provide harmonious music. The pleasing effect of music depends on melody, rhythm and harmony.

Not all audible sounds are pleasing to the ear, and hence sounds used in music are those which individually and collectively appeal to the ear and the intellect. Different notes produced from a source can either be in consonance or discordant. Ancients discovered consonance and realised that there are degrees of consonance in relation to a reference note. Perfect consonance or unison occurs when both sounds have the same pitch, or the second note is a multiplier of the frequency of the first. The second note is then referred to as an octave of the first. The other notes which have lesser degrees of consonance with the reference note also have some degree of identity with it. From time immemorial people have recognised this fact and employed it in their musical systems.

These notes with lesser consonance also bear a mathematical relationship with the reference note. Where the two octaves have been interspersed with new notes at an incremental of one fifth the reference note's frequency, a system of pentatonic scale evolved as is evident in Chinese and African music. In India and in Greece, the octaves were interspersed with two extra notes, which were in ratios of four is to three with the octave thus creating the diatonic scale. The seven notes of the Pythogorean scale were used in Greek music and formed the basis of the six Greek modes. These modes resemble some of the 'that's' of Indian classical music. Two of the Greek modes were adopted by Western music in the seventeenth century and are now referred to as the 'major' and the 'minor' scales. Indian music adopted the diatonic scale similar to the Western 'major' scale, and both possibly share a common remote origin.

In the Western music, every note in a scale is fixed and is of a particular frequency, where as in Indian music, though the relationship between the notes remain the same, the note themselves can have varying frequencies. In addition to the seven pure notes, there are five altered notes in the Indian octave. Ragas are the discernible melodic forms underlying all Indian classical music. 'Ragas' depict moods and evolved over centuries. Students learnt from their teachers by hearing and practising. Music was a closely guarded secret only passed on to a few favourite students, thus no written record of music was kept. Musicologists in the twentieth century tried to classify Ragas. The sheer volume of 'Ragas' defy logical classification. However some musicologists, Bhatkhande in particular, grouped 'Ragas' into 'Thats' according to the notes used and other variations. Though it is not a perfect classification, at least it manages to place most of them in groups obeying certain rules.

Shridhar had told her that a 'Raga' cannot be identified by reading about it. It has to be heard many times, and then it becomes easily discernible. Our brain obviously has an area of pitch perception and recognition which transcends the physical aspects of intonation. Mind has considerable latitude in the comprehension of music intervals, and variations in intonation by different singers did not change the 'Raga' form and is easily perceived by the brain.

At first Rini did not understand half of what Shridhar was telling her. But over the years as she immersed herself in classical Indian music she perceived the truth, and having gained insight into 'Raga' music she began to enjoy it. When she practised, at times she lost track of time floating down the world of pitch rhythm and harmony. A door to a new world was opened to her, where she would often escape. It was a world of pleasure, a world of creativity and a world uniquely her own.

There are anecdotes and legends about past masters in the art of 'Raga' music. In the middle ages, Emperor Akbar was a connoisseur of art and learning. Mia Tansen was a court singer, and it is said that once while singing 'Raga-Deepak', set fire to himself. A friend of his had to douse him with water to save his life. In a historic marathon singing contest between Tansen and Baiju Bawra, the wild animals from the forest were attracted to the palace. Baiju Bawra apparently melted a stone with his voice. It is very unlikely that anyone with such vocal prowess lives in this century. Legends have a way of blurring the truth, and today it is impossible to sift between the facts and exaggeration. We have moved away from nature; perhaps that is why in today's world our voice fails to resonate with nature.

Shridhar encouraged Rini to listen to all kinds of music: from western masters to pop singers of this century, Indian folk songs, film songs, and different forms of melody. To him music is pleasing sound expressing human emotions, and he wanted Rini to think and perceive outside the prescriptive world of classical music. He often gave the example of Tagore, the Nobel laureate Bengali poet, who had the courage to experiment with music, and was the first to try and fuse melodies of different geographical and scholastic origins. Shridhar would often impress upon Rini that listening to the wider spectrum will broaden her approach and understanding of music.

Rini looked at her wristwatch. It was only two in the afternoon. The warm Sun on this cold December day was pleasantly intoxicating and exhilarating. She ambled through Janpath, leisurely taking in the sight sound and smell of this unfamiliar city. The hawkers and the tourists; the incessant noise of the traffic; the moving mosaic of dappled shadow of the high leaf-less branches on the marble pavement, tarnished with dust and dead leaves. Stray dogs were casting lazy eyes on the passers by hopeful of some discarded food. She was thankful that playback singers could remain anonymous in a crowded street unlike film stars who invariably create civil disturbances and traffic jams, with their God-like hold on the population.

Her mind drifted back over the years, and she had the strange out of body sensation, as she saw in her mind's eye the events that twisted and turned her life, made her what she is: her childhood, the awful accident, her desire to die when they gave up searching for Rajiv and declared him dead, buried under tons of rock in the freezing water of Alaknanda; Dadaji's kindness and patience that eventually brought her round; and then the struggle. First it was learning to walk using her crutches, and then to forget the past and to make a niche for herself in the world, to strive towards a future. Is her struggle over yet? And if it is over, then what will she live for? As long as Dadaji is around, she has an anchor, and then what? Since achieving material success, these thoughts have been troubling her more and more. Dadaji had suggested marriage, but she will have nothing to do with it. Whenever she thinks of Rajiv, she still hurts, may be not as incessantly as before, but every lonely moment: every shared laughter, every face that looks familiar brings back the events on her mind's screen, and she re-lives the tragedy. It has now become bearable with the passage of time, and she no longer bursts into tears. She knows that she will not be able to share her mind with any one else, the most important ingredient towards a happy family life.

She stumbled on something soft and a sharp yelp of pain and annoyance brought her back to reality. She had kicked a stray, basking in the winter Sun. With a show of displeasure and with obvious reluctance the half-starved dog slunk away. She looked around for 'Kashmir Emporium'. She was looking for a particular dress and a warm shawl for Dadaji. Not seeing the shop, she asked directions from one of the street vendors. Making sure that she understood the directions, she retraced her steps the way she had come and looking for landmarks made her way towards the shop.

The shop was fairly crowded with tourists, looking at exquisitely carved wooden and stone artwork on display. Some were taken up with the embroidered shawls and jackets. Rini joined this group, and flipped through the hanging suits. There was a lovely yellow one. Yellow used to be her favourite colour, but since the accident, when she was wearing a yellow garhwali dress, she flinches from that colour. She selected an olive green dress suit and a greyish white embroidered shawl for Dadaji and left the shop. A quick glance at her watch showed the time to be half past three. She wanted to reach the hotel by five, to have enough time for a bath and dress up at leisure. After aimless walking in the Connaught place, window shopping, and having a plate of Bhel-puri, she called an auto rickshaw to take her back to the hotel. Dadaji had insisted on coming to New Delhi with her, and would be amongst the audience. He is getting old now, and can sometimes be very child-like and obstinate.

Reaching the hotel, Rini paid off the auto rickshaw. She checked up on Dadaji to make sure he was all right, and gave him the shawl overcoming his anticipated protests. She then made her way to her own room. She flung the purchases on the bed, took out the dress she was going to wear that evening, her jewellery box and the make-up kit. She arranged them carefully near the dressing table, undressed and turned on the taps of the bath.

Rini luxuriated in the warm scented bath water and closing her eyes, let her mind drift off to ruminate the past. She watched the nervous young girl walk up to the stage and adjust the microphone. The music system in the background started to play the music, and taking her cue the girl started to sing. It was a hesitant start, but with the flow of the music her confidence grew. She left the judges and the audience far behind and drifted into her own world. As the last beats of the music died down, a thunderous applause greeted her, dragging her back to reality. She had lived that event many times in her mind, but never tired of seeing it again and again. That was the first step towards the success that awaited her. She was selected to move on to the next round of the television reality show competition for budding playback singers.

Rini dressed quickly and put on her make up. Throwing a quick critical eye at the image in the mirror, Rini turned and walked to the table to sort out the music sheets scattered on it. In her haste she dropped something metallic that hit the floor with a tinkle. Making an explosive sound of annoyance she went on her hands and knees to recover the item. It was a brooch that she was presented with for participating in the television reality show. She picked it up, and slowly stood up. A flood of memory swept through her mind: Rakesh was one of the programme directors at Shimla radio station, and after her first recording had suggested that she should participate in the television reality show where aspiring playback singers will have to compete to win the coveted singer of the year award. Rini was not very keen, but Shridhar and Shukra were quite excited by the idea, and the up shot of it was that she found herself going for the audition.

Rini was invited to Mumbai for the contest. It was a talent search competition, where participants had to sing live on stage, and a combination of judges' marks and audience vote ensured passage to the next round. There were a hundred participants, and gradually over the next few weeks they were whittled down to ten. At first Rini was nervous and stiff, but the excitement of singing in front of live audience, and the applause soon dissipated her fears. She had enjoyed herself. She had received favourable comments from all the judges, but was voted out of the contest. She was a bit disappointed, especially after spending weeks and months of effort. She learnt a lot as well. All the contestants received professional advice on mike handling, voice throwing and stagecraft. They learnt to entertain and engage the crowd not only through their voice, but their body movements as well. They received professional coaching and advice.

Before she left Mumbai she received an offer to record a playback song for a Bollywood film. She had received a modest retainer for her efforts. It was a catchy tune, but she did not think much of it at the time. Six months later when that album was released however, that song was a hit. Overnight she started receiving offers for playback singing and live concerts. She had a few successes and a steady income. Quite often she had to fly to Mumbai where most of the recordings were done. Dadaji was her constant companion and source of courage and inspiration. Tonight's concert was a charity event. The organisers had pledged to donate all the money raised to the orphanage for destitute girls and women. This was a charity close to

Rini's heart, and she had no hesitation in accepting the invitation. She was told to expect three hundred guests and all seats were taken. The concert was to be held in the banquet hall of the hotel. She looked at her watch. It was time to go.

THE CONCERT

Rajiv entered the lobby of the hotel. The dazzle of the chandeliers' light reflected off the marble floor and granite walls and the mirrors were in stark contrast to the subdued lighting of the driveway. He had to blink his eyes to get used to the brightness. He looked around to orient himself and locate the Banquet Hall. His sweeping gaze took in a well-dressed pleasant young lady coming out of the lift. She looked familiar. As she raised her head, their eyes met and held. She faltered in her step. Following a brief hesitation, with staring eyes, parted lips and colour draining off her face, she shrieked and ran straight at him, and into his arms. She hugged him tightly, and his arms went round her automatically. She was weeping uncontrollably, spoiling his best suit. He looked around for support, and racked his brains to remember her—all to no avail. He was stumped. How do you ask a young lady in your arms, obviously in a heightened emotional state, who she was! Obviously she either knew him very well, or had mistaken him for someone else. Then there was this nagging feeling that this probably was the same girl he saw in his dreams that invariably turned into a recurring nightmares. He took the bull by the horn, inhaled deeply, and said, "I have seen you so many times in my dreams. Your laughter and your singing and your impish expressions were so real to me, and then the dream would turn into a nightmare—I am falling, falling . . . . and so cold, so intensely unbelievably cold. I wake up bathed in sweat and shiver. I must have had an accident." He paused, "You know, I cannot remember anything before that period. I feel it deep within myself that I know you well, yet I cannot remember your name. Please, will you tell me who you are, and what is our relationship?"

Rini lifted her head off his chest and tilted her face to look at him, but the rivulets of tears running down her cheek blurred her vision and prevented her from seeing the gentle smile playing on his lips. She gave up, and once again buried her head against his chest, and if anything, tightened her grip on him. He stood there in the middle of the lobby holding an uncontrollably weeping young woman, tightly embracing him. People around them had stopped to stare, but they were oblivious to the world, lost in the bliss of finding each other, and that is how Dadaji found them a few minutes later.